BEWITCHED BY THE ALPHA

by: Bryce Evans

Copyright © October 2015 Bryce Evans
Art and Logo Copyright © Bryce Evans

All rights reserved.

Edited by: Alexis Arendt
Artwork by: Jess Buffett
Formatted by: Stacey Price
Published by: Bryce Evans

E-books are not transferrable.

This book is intended for the purchaser's sole use.
Sharing, or downloading to other individuals or devices is illegal.
This work is fictional. Any resemblance to real persons, places, or events is purely coincidental.

All Rights Are Reserved.

No part of this book may be used or reproduced in any manner whatsoever without written permission of the author, except in the case of quotations embodied in critical articles and reviews.

Dedication

I would like to acknowledge my mom, who passed away a few years ago; she told me to follow my dreams and never allow anyone to tell me I couldn't achieve them.

Thanks to the love of my life, John, for making me a place to write and even taking up the slack when I was typing away in my own world. You helped to make my dream come true. It may be a small table in the corner, but it's my corner of make believe, where dreams do come true.

Thanks to my beautiful kids, who keep me grounded and drive me crazy at the same time. I love you all.

Thanks to Janka Dustan, who agreed to be my PA and tells me now what to do and when to do it. We have been figuring it out and having a great time at it. Thanks, Janka for all of your help and kindness.

A special thanks to my friend Bobbi Kinion, who beta reads and gives me great advice. Also, thank you to all of my Nite Stalkers who have stood behind me throughout the good and bad times. Thank you, Bobbi Kinion, Kent Kinion, Kristina Galbert, Janka Dustan, Amy Bowens, Sara Gomez, Lori Backfire Twardokus, Ronda Reed, Debbie Raddatz, Lori Engelbrektso, Penny DeLoche, Christine Lease Wheeling, Tina Brunelle, Rachel Harrington, Cindy Harris, Kelley Hopkins, Helly Kasprzak, Carolyn Hall Brown, Kerry Anne Porter, and Pamela Altman Talley.

Thanks to the Bryce Evans Paranormal Society, who have helped me spread the word of my books and keep driving me.

A SPECIAL THANKS to the REBELS. You know who you are.

It's a long road but it's worth it! We did it!!!!!!

Please be kind and leave a review on the site you purchased the book from.

Blurb

A Heartbreaking Tragedy can bring a weary soul New Hope.

After a lifetime of guilt over his mother's death, Arden Dixon has grown weary of the push and pull on his soul as the Alpha of the Dixon Pack. It seems he's forever playing peacemaker, and protecting the innocent. When he finds a beautiful woman in the midst of a painful transition, he realizes that his fate lies in her hands.

The Wrong Place At The Wrong Time Quinn wanted nothing more than to live her solitary life in peace selling her treasures in her own store, but a brutal attack by a wolf has given her no choice but to embrace a new family and a new way of life. That doesn't mean she has to embrace the whole mating thing though, right?

New Hope
A man with a need to protect, and a woman with a desire to stand on her own. Can these two souls find peace in each other, or will the brutality of their circumstances break them for good?

Prologue

He didn't notice he'd picked up a tail on his jog until he heard the pattering of feet hitting the leaves behind him. Whoever it was meant to make enough noise to be heard. He decided to pick up his speed and see if they could keep up, but the sound only got closer. Finley's mind flashed back to the war in Afghanistan, and being followed while on patrol. His adrenaline picked up, making him run faster. The trail for Arden Dixon's land was just ahead; maybe he could lose them there. But even as he made the turn, he could still hear the crunching steps of his pursuers.

As he rounded the curve, he found a big red wolf blocking his path. He'd lived in New Hope all his life, and was used to seeing wolves and bears in the woods, but this wolf was different. In fact, he looked like he had rabies. His fur was matted together in places, with black smudges all over it. He wasn't foaming at the mouth, but the crazed light in his eyes stopped Finley dead in his tracks. Finley knew when a predator was getting ready to attack, and the wolf in front of him was crouched down, clearly ready to spring.

He knew he couldn't outrun the animal, so he needed to show it that he wasn't afraid. That was the only chance he had of coming out of this alive. The wind blew against his face, and the scent of rotten eggs traveled up his nose. Slowly he reached down and picked up a large stick lying by the side of the path.

That's when he noticed the others. A pack of wolves standing quietly by, watching him. *Shit*, he thought. If he were facing a man, he could handle that, but a freaking pack of wolves was something different.

Finley held the stick like a bat, getting ready for a fight. He had to turn sideways in order to keep all the wolves in his sights. The ones at his back were coming a little too close, and he had no choice but to swing the stick.

Bingo. He hit one of the wolves, slamming it backwards into the dirt, but then another one charged him. He had to swing to kill, because these wolves clearly meant to make a meal out of him. He was getting ready for another hit when he felt the sharp fangs of the wolf in front of him sink into his calf muscle. If he jerked away, the beast could take a big chunk out of his leg.

He swung the limb with his other arm, but before he could make contact the wolf had let go and backed off. In fact, they were all backing away from him. Shocking him further, when they'd all moved a few feet back then laid down on the ground.

The pain of the bite was searing. He must have rabies, because there was no other reason for the wound to hurt that bad. His calf muscle was still intact; his only injuries were the puncture wounds from the wolf's fangs. Nothing else.

Suddenly all the wolves stood up and ran into the woods. Finley shook his head. For a moment it was as if he could hear a voice talking to him. He shook his head again, trying to clear the words from his mind. The wolf must've had rabies; that, or the doctors were correct and he was having some kind of PTSD flashback.

*****

Silas and Hannah Hoffman shifted behind the trees and watched as the man moaned in pain as the change started to take affect.

"It won't be long before we have what we need, Sister," Silas whispered. Both could hear the Dixon pack coming in the distance. "This couldn't have turned out better."

Hannah smiled. "So it begins."

Chapter 1

Arden waited for Charley to shift, but he couldn't. The little guy was thinking too hard. He watched as the little boy struggled, eventually getting so frustrated that he gave up and stomped off, crying.

He waited, giving the boy plenty of warning that he was coming up behind him. He didn't say anything until Charley finally spoke. "Why can't I shift like the rest, Alpha?"

Arden smiled, and then patted the ground beside him. Charley walked over and sat down. The kid was breaking his heart as tears fell from his eyes. Arden knew he was considered the runt out of all the kids, and the most picked on.

"I'll tell you a secret Charley, but you have to join the Little Mites first."

Charley's eyes sparked with interest as he turned to face his Alpha. "Who are the Little Mites?"

"Well, you see Charley, I was a Little Mite. When I was your age, a group of us formed our own club. It was me, Bane, Tate, and a few others who couldn't shift the first time. Man, we got made fun of for a whole week. While everyone else went off and shifted, we went down to our clubhouse and hid out. My dad found us about two weeks later. He'd been so busy that he didn't know that we hadn't shifted and should've been at class learning to be a wolf. I was the Alpha's son, so I was expected to be the best, but I was having a hard time."

"Just like me," Charley said.

"Yep, just like you."

"But…but how did you become Alpha if you couldn't shift?" Charley asked.

"Remember, Charley, you have to keep this secret. Only the Little Mites know this secret, and only members know how to get people to shift. So if you want to be a member, then you have to hold up your right hand and repeat after me," Arden told him seriously. He waited for Charley to sit up straight and raise his right hand. "I, Charley Nathaniel Ripken, do solemnly swear to protect all those who are weaker than me, and to keep the secrets of the Little Mites and only pass them on to someone else who is in need just like me." Arden leaned forward. "Say 'I swear.'"

"I swear," Charley repeated.

"I promise to train every day and never make fun of anyone bigger or smaller than me, and to always help those in need," Arden continued. "And I promise to obey my parents and Alpha, and to do all my chores without any objections." Arden watched as Charley narrowed his eyes in surprise at the last part. "Come on now, say 'I promise.'"

"I promise, Alpha."

"Then I now declare you a member of the Little Mites. Congratulations, Charley."

Charley's smile was so big; Arden thought the kid's face was going to crack.

"Alpha, I still haven't shifted yet." Charley's smile faded as he thought about it.

"Do you trust your Alpha, Charley?"

"Of course I do."

"Then I want you to close your eyes, and when I describe something I want you to think about it and then reach out and touch it. Do you understand?"

Charley nodded and closed his eyes.

"Remember last fall when we had the October fest and we let all of you guys run with the wolves?" Charley smiled again, and nodded. "That was a fun time, wasn't it Charley?"

"Yes sir, it was the best."

"Do you remember when I shifted and ran up to you guys and you all rubbed your hands up and down my fur? I want you to reach out, Charley, and pet my fur." Arden let himself partially shift. His arms sprouted hair as Charley reached out. Arden stuck his arm underneath the boy's hand so he could feel it. "Now Charley, I want you to think about your fur and how it feels on your wolf. You feel your wolf inside of you?"

Charley continued to rub Arden's arm, then started smiling. Arden knew that he could feel his wolf. His skin was starting to ripple, and he needed just a little more to push him over. "Call to your wolf, Charley. Let him out to feel the wind blowing through his hair. Jump over those logs. Do you feel the pads of your paws hitting the ground? Your Alpha is waiting to run with you. Shift now, Charley. Shift." And just like that, Charley shredded his clothes and shifted into his wolf.

"You've done it, Charley! Great job. Now let's go have some fun. Run with your Alpha."

Arden shifted and took off running. He could hear Charley behind him as they ran toward the other pups. He slowed down, allowing the boy to run beside him as they came upon the clearing where everyone was playing. The others stopped and stared, watching Charley as he ran beside the Alpha. It was a big thing to be able to run with him, and now Charley was the big man among the pups. Well, Little Mite, but he wore it with honor.

Even the bigger kids came up to him, and they all started playing. What Charley didn't know was that Arden had used the same words his father used on him. He was a man with a lot of wisdom, and Arden missed him, especially at times like this. Watching the pups brought a sense of purpose to his life. He hoped that one day he would be able to watch his own pups when it was their time.

*****

Arden Dixon couldn't shake the feeling that today wasn't going to be a good day, even though the birds were chirping outside and all that crap. He took one look at his Beta as he walked into his office and knew he was right. Today was going to be a shit day.

"How bad is it?" Arden asked, leaning back in his chair.

"Not good." Bane Cross sat down in the chair across from his Alpha. His blond hair looked disheveled as he ran his fingers through it. "Another human was bitten last night. We got to him before they carried him off, and he's in confinement until he gets through the change."

"Who is it this time?" Arden asked. He stood up, walked over to the window, and stared out at the lake, watching as ducks landed on the water. He wanted to go outside and stretch his legs, and shift. The vague sense of doom he felt wasn't going away, though, and he was needed here.

When he looked back, Bane had leaned forward; his blue frosty eyes flickered with anger before he answered. "Finley Egan, the police chief's son."

Arden swung around abruptly. "Fuck. They have to be targeting certain people. Finley is strong, and he just got back from the military. He must have been picked because of that."

Max Conell, Alpha of the Conell pack, had sent out a message to the surrounding towns that a rogue pack was targeting humans. Two humans had been attacked; one hadn't made it through the change. On that occasion there was a witness who told Max what had happened. Max explained that two friends had broken down on the side of the highway and were attacked by a pack of wolves. One of the boys had a rifle with him, and he killed one of the wolves. The rest of the pack ran off, but unfortunately the other boy was bitten. Max didn't have a clue why, but once the boy started going through the change, he died.

"We need to find out who the hell is doing this before the Council sends *them*." There were times he hated the Council. They were a group of Alphas, made up of wolves, bears, witches, and wizards. There was even a vampire on it. He'd never seen the man himself, but Arden knew he was over five hundred years old.

Bane's eyes narrowed. "Who?"

With forced calm, Arden said, "The Death Hunters." Everyone had heard of the Death Hunters. Their name sent chills up a wolf's spine when it was mentioned. When a problem became too much for a pack, or any paranormal family to handle, the Council would send in the Death Hunters.

Most of the time the Council was fair, but sending the Death Hunters out would only make his pack remember what had happened to his mom and dad. It was a glimpse of his past that he didn't want to be brought up again. The Hunters were appropriately named; they brought nothing with them but death.

Just their name brought back horrible memories. A local witch who lived in their town had cast a spell on his father, forcing him to shift into his wolf, and then kill his only son—Arden. Arden's mother got between them before he could succeed, and Arden's father ended up killing her instead.

Arden was still a child when all that happened, but it felt like yesterday. The Death Hunters had been sent by the Council to resolve the matter, and they had decided to kill both the witch and Arden's father.

His father had been a good wolf. The witch had acted out of revenge; Arden's father had refused to change her daughter into a werewolf. It was forbidden to do such a thing; only human mates were lawfully permitted to be changed. The girl had been distraught, and killed herself on the pack's land, leaving a note that said it was his father's fault.

Ever since then, Arden had hated witches, and Death Hunters. He'd been left without a mother or father, and that pain and anger hadn't faded with time.

Arden shook his head to try to drive the thoughts from it. "Let's gather the pack and meet. I want them to be on the lookout for anyone strange in our territory. Tonight after the meeting we go out and patrol. I'll go with you to town; maybe we'll get lucky," Arden said. Bane nodded and left.

Arden needed to find out who was doing this, in a hurry. If humans found out they were being targeted, it would be a disaster for relations between the town and the pack. Most of the town folk knew about his kind, and so far they'd stayed on a common ground. They helped each other out when they needed to. When young kids got lost, it was pack members who found them. Pack members owned most of the town, which kept the town in jobs. It was an important balance, and Arden couldn't allow anything to damage it.

Plus, the Council would think he couldn't handle it and send in the Death Hunters, and nobody wanted that.

Now he needed to go and talk to Deaton Egan, the police chief. Deaton was a good man, and knew about his pack. They worked together whenever they had a problem arise, and most of the time he allowed Arden to handle problems regarding his pack. But this was different; Finley was the chief's only son. Not a lot of new people moved to their town, mainly because it was so small, but it was close enough to the city to bring in customers to the country store and Charlotte's Closet. New Hope was famous for its wildlife, and there were strict laws against hunting here. The woods were packed with tourists who came for the nature walks.

Laughter brought him from his deep thoughts as the pups ran by his window. He waved and smiled, and Charley stood up straighter, puffing his chest out. He held the confidence that he needed, now.

Arden would have loved to join in their play, but he had a lot to do. First he needed to check on Finley and see how he was doing.

Eventually Finley's father would be allowed to see him, but how soon depended on how well Finley's body was accepting the change. Arden had known Finley since he was born, and now he was a strapping twenty-seven year-old Marine. Arden needed to make sure he was okay.

Chapter 2

Arden walked into the pack house, not expecting to see so many of his wolves gathered there. Most of them had jobs, and yet here they were in the middle of the afternoon. Something was wrong, and he didn't like the fact that he was apparently the last to know.

"Bane?" Arden yelled out. He watched as the members all lowered their eyes, showed him their necks, and bowed as he walked past them. Not one of them made eye contact with their Alpha. Everyone knew Deaton, and now his son was one of them. It had to be strange having the police chief's son here in the pack house, the one place where they could usually be themselves and not hide from anyone. Finley Egan being a turned wolf would bring unwanted attention to the pack.

He loved this house. They'd built it for the pack members who weren't mated yet. They'd built it approximately five years ago and everyone in the pack contributed to it. They cut the logs themselves, put up every wall, and put in the plumbing and electricity.

Someone was always cooking something sweet in the kitchen; even now he could smell banana-nut bread cooking. The kitchen was outfitted with the finest appliances, including a stainless steel stove and refrigerator. It was a cook's dream kitchen. He made sure this house had everything a wolf or human could want, including a mudroom with a dog door big enough for a wolf to get through. The house was built for wolves with tempers, and young pups who didn't know their own strength. Most of the walls were sturdy enough that even a wolf couldn't kick a hole in them.

He and all his command staff, including the guards, had one wing of the house to themselves. They shared a joint living area and a kitchen, but other than that it was quieter on his side of the house.

"Alpha, I'm in here," Bane answered, standing next to the door to Finley's room.

"What's wrong?" Arden demanded.

"Nothing's wrong, it's just...unusual." Bane was peering through the window in the door.

"What is?"

"I've never seen anyone change so quickly. I would've thought the full moon tonight would have pulled it out of him, but look for yourself." Bane backed up so Arden could look through the glass. Inside Finley Egan was leaning back in a chair, his feet kicked up on the table, watching the TV as if he didn't have a care in the world. But as Arden looked closer he could see the tick in Finley's jaw.

Finley Egan was huge, and now that he'd made the change he looked even bigger. Those who hadn't seen Finley since he got back from the military might've thought that the military had put the extra muscle on him, but Arden knew it was the wolf inside him. Every human who changed would show an increase in muscle mass, and more extras than they could ever wish for. They would be stronger, faster, and able to scent and see better than any human. Finley's blond hair had grown out a bit, and was sticking up like he'd just run his fingers in it. Even though he was acting calm, Arden could see the wildness waiting to jump through. It took great control to keep it under, but if Finley didn't get it out soon, they would have a pissed off Alpha wolf on their hands—because it was obvious from Finley's size and control that he was definitely an Alpha.

Arden could see the Marine tattoo peaking through the bottom of his shirt. Finley had seen action while he was on active duty, and had lost a lot of friends. His body might look in good shape, but Finley's eyes showed the war raging as his wolf fought to break free within him.

"How do you know he's changed already?" Arden asked, his eyes never leaving his newest pack member.

"I watched him change, and then I ordered him to change back and he did." Bane snapped his fingers. "Just like that. I've never seen anyone but you change that fast."

"And you too, Bane." But Bane was right; it was strange. His Beta was an Alpha himself, and could easily have his own pack, but he chose to stay with his best friend. Arden thanked his lucky stars every day for that. Bane said he loved his pack and he liked being Beta, so it worked for the both of them.

Apparently, Finley had been an Alpha in his human life and it carried over with him. The question Arden needed an answer to was whether Finley could be part of the pack, or would he challenge Arden constantly? Arden had a lot of challenges under his belt, but Finley was strong, and he knew how to win.

"Was he this calm after he changed?" Arden asked, looking up at his Beta.

"Actually, he was excited and wanted to go and run in the woods. I know we're prohibited from changing anyone against their will, but Finley doesn't seem to mind much." Bane answered. "He acts like he's enjoying this, and that's what's worrying me."

"Open the door." Arden stepped back to allow Bane to unlock the door and then walked inside. Finley glanced up at him, but didn't move. Arden could see in Finley's grey eyes that he was a predator. He showed no signs of being frightened of Arden, but watched him closely as he sat down in the chair across from him.

"Finley, how are you feeling?" Arden asked.

"Strong," Finley answered. Arden couldn't tell if the man was fucking with him or not.

"I'm going to see your dad in a few minutes and tell him what happened. I'm sorry about this. We don't go around biting humans. It's not sanctioned, and I'll need to get some information from you, if you can remember anything about the wolves who did this to you." Arden noticed that Finley continued to stare at him. His father used to do that to him, to see if he could make Arden look away. It hadn't worked on him then, either. He had the feeling that Finley was testing him. "That won't work on me."

"What won't work on you?" Finley asked.

"The staring. I'm an Alpha, son, and I have the feeling you are too. I know that all your emotions are wreaking havoc in your body right now, but most young wolves don't test the Alpha the way you are, unless they want their ass kicked. Right now, I don't know if you even realize what you're doing, though."

Finley blinked a couple of times, then looked away from Arden and back again. "I'm pissed right now about getting my rights taken away from me. My father told me about werewolves, but I assumed the old man was getting a little nuts. I thought for sure he was crazy, but I was the one who was wrong. I guess I never thought that it could be true, but I feel all this power inside of me, and it feels good. I'm trying to control it, but it's taking a lot out of me. Why do I want to hit something, tear something up, run as fast as I can? Shit, I feel like I could take on the world."

"That's natural for a new wolf after their first shift. You're an adult, and you're an Alpha, which makes you stronger. When we get you in the woods you'll want to fight anyone—or fuck anyone who suits your fancy. But believe me, this is normal Finley. We'll help you get through it. That's what a pack is for. I need you to trust me right now, son, and believe that I will help you learn to live with this."

Arden watched as the far off look came into Finley's eyes. "I remember a pack of wolves surrounding me on my jog. I tried to outrun them, and when I figured out that I couldn't, I picked up a stick and started swinging. Fuckers surrounded me, and then the leader of the pack came up behind me while I was focused on the others. The fucker bit into my leg, then sat down and waited. I couldn't believe they didn't attack when my leg went out from under me. I lay there waiting, but they all just lay down on the ground watching me. It was the biggest one who bit me."

"How many wolves surrounded you?" Arden leaned forward.

"About five or seven, I think. Some of them were behind the pack, but they were the smaller wolves. At first I thought I got bit by a wolf with rabies, because the pain was so bad." Finley shook his head. "I've been shot before and I didn't hurt like that."

Arden chuckled. "That's the change. It's not meant to be fun. Some don't make it; only the strong ones survive. And the wolves in the back were the females and kids of the pack. They're not allowed to fight; in fact, I wonder why they were there at all. No pack should allow their females and kids to go out hunting with them. They should be tucked away safely in their home territory. You've probably noticed that no females or kids have been around since you've been here. They've been kept away from the pack house for safety reasons until you've gotten adjusted to your new body. Bane said that you've already shifted and then changed back. That's unheard of except for an Alpha, and from what I'm seeing you're definitely an Alpha. You're stronger than most of the wolves, so be careful because you can hurt those who are smaller and weaker than you. You have a lot of strength flowing through your body right now."

"You're not worried about me trying to hurt you?" Finley asked. Arden could tell that Finley was a good man who only wanted answers; he wasn't trying to be threatening.

"Nope. You're strong, don't get me wrong, but not stronger than me yet. I've lived a long time, Finley, and I haven't stayed Alpha this long without knowing how to fight. I know you do too, but this will be different for you. I'll help you control those raging emotions you're feeling, but nothing happens overnight. I'm asking for you to trust me that I'll get you through this. So what do you say?"

Finley stayed silent, but Arden knew that he was thinking carefully about it, and that said a lot about the Alpha Finley was going to be.

"I trust you, but you've got to get me out of this room soon and let me box a little, or run. I've got to get rid of some of this energy."

"You got it. I'm going to see your dad, then tonight we'll run. Try to rest until then." Arden chuckled when he saw Finley's expression.

"Rest? Hell I'm doing good not running around the room a hundred times."

"Then do it. Do as many push-ups and sit-ups as you can do, and then when you feel like taking a nap, do it. Someone's cooking now, and you need to eat. Your body is burning a lot of calories just sitting there, and when you run around and exercise you'll be starving. So pack on the food." Arden got up and walked out of the room. He had a father to see, and he wasn't looking forward to it.

Chapter 3

Arden drove out of pack territory with Bane and his cousin Tate Dixon, who was his head enforcer. It was starting to get dark by the time they arrived in town. Not a lot of people were around, since Charlotte's Closet had closed down last month. They used to get a lot of business from the larger city people wanting to stay at Charlotte's bed and breakfast and then shop at her store. Since her husband died, she couldn't run both the store and bed and breakfast. She'd told Arden that she was tired of trying to find the right items to sell in the store, so she'd put the store up for sale and decided to just run the bed and breakfast, which she was great at. The woman could cook, and customers came back year after year.

They needed to get more shops in town, so they didn't have to go so far to get supplies. It was early fall, and since Charlotte closed her store the town looked a little sad. It was like a ghost town, with all the lights off and the clothes out of the windows. Charlotte's Closet had been the biggest store in town, with all kinds of clothes and knickknacks. Now they would have to order things online, or go to the city, and Arden hated going out of town.

Bane had called Chief Egan earlier to see when he would be at his office. He'd had to take a prisoner to the next county over for court, so they'd made an appointment to see him at eight o'clock that evening.

Tate's stomach growled as they pulled into town. "I'm starving," he complained.

Arden and Bane laughed, because Tate was always hungry. The man was six-foot-five, and at least two hundred and sixty pounds. Not one ounce of fat graced the wolf's body—he was nothing but powerful, ripped muscles.

They passed Charlotte's Closet, and noticed that the "For Sale" sign had been taken down and clothing had been placed on the mannequins in the store windows. Apparently Charlotte had found a buyer. He needed to talk to her to see who she'd sold it to.

"Charlotte must've sold the store. She didn't tell me. Wonder what's going on?" Arden mumbled. He'd just spoken with her two days ago. In fact, he'd been thinking of buying it himself, for any pack member who wanted to start a business in it.

"Shit, my fault, Alpha. She called the office a couple days ago, but with everything going on with the rogues, I forgot to tell you. She said she sold it to a nice lady who already had a clothing business online and wanted to find a nice town to settle down in. Charlotte couldn't pass up the money she was offering. What was the woman's name?" Bane closed his eyes, thinking. "Quinn something."

"Her name is Quinn?" Tate asked, laughing.

"Yep. I thought it was cool, that's why I remember her first name, but the last name is funny-sounding and of course it popped right out of my head." Bane chuckled.

Arden snorted. "Did you at least do a background check on her?"

"Started it, Alpha, but I haven't checked my e-mail for it yet." Bane cringed at his mistake. "Sorry. I'm off my game with all this going on. I'll check it at the restaurant."

Arden just nodded. They were all off their game. He needed to find out what the hell this pack was doing, and get rid of it. He could feel in his bones that things were going to get worse before it got better.

"Send it to my e-mail too. I want to see who this Quinn is." He wanted to find out as much as he could about any newcomers.

The window did look pretty cool. Tate slowed down as they passed, so they could all look inside. Whoever this Quinn was, she knew how to attract attention. Fall was here, and the store reminded him of his childhood, when he and his mom would help decorate the whole town.

The kids loved it. Hell, *he* loved it. Pumpkins and fall decorations adorned the windows, and even the outside of the shop.

Apparently she was going to have a variety of items in the store. He could see men's, women's, and children's mannequins dressed up. It looked like there were purses and jewelry on the walls and tables, along with candles and other decorative items. It all looked great; he could almost smell the mulled cider heating on the stove.

"Alright, let's go eat before we have to deal with Deaton," Arden said as Tate drove past the store and parked behind the police station. They'd started walking toward Mick's restaurant when they heard a growl and the clang of something slamming into some trashcans. Arden was already running toward the back of Charlotte's Closet when a woman started screaming.

Arden came to a stop and watched a woman slam her fist into the side of the wolf's head. He knew that this was the pack he was looking for. There were only two wolves there, including the Alpha. He started moving again, but before he could get to the woman the wolf latched onto her arm and bit down, releasing his saliva into her wound.

"You fucking piece of shit," the woman yelled out, kicking the wolf until it released her. By the time Arden reached her, the wolves had run away.

"I've got her. Try to find them," Arden yelled at Bane and Tate, who shifted and ran after the wolves.

The sight of Bane and Tate shifting caused the woman to go deathly still. Her eyes widened, and she crab-walked away from Arden, but she wasn't quick enough to get away before Arden leaned down beside her.

Putting her hands up, she yelled, "You get away from me!"

"I just want to help you." Arden stopped when he got a good look at the woman. His heart actually jumped. She was very beautiful, and very angry.

Fiery red hair hung down her back, but it was her piercing green eyes that grabbed his soul. It was those green eyes that grew angrier from the moment she focused on him, burning with fire as he came closer. All he wanted to do was comfort her. She looked scared, even though she hid it well with her fury.

"You're just like them. What, you want to bite my other arm now?" The woman tried to get up, but just then the transition started taking affect. "Fuckkkk." She grabbed her stomach and curled into a ball on the ground, whimpering. The change was happening fast.

"Breathe in and out and it will pass in a few minutes." Arden put his arm around her and picked her up. "What's your name?"

"My name's Quinn. What did he do to me? Oh my God, do I have rabies?"

Arden smiled and chuckled. "No. I'll explain when I get you in the car." He couldn't keep his eyes off her, but the moment he glanced up, she unleashed a punch to his nose, surprising him enough to loosen his grip on her. This gave her enough time to jump out of his arms and take off running toward the woods.

Arden reached up to touch his nose and found it bleeding. He smiled as he watched the woman whirl back around when Tate emerged from the woods in wolf form.

"I think I'm in love." She'd hit him hard, and it should've pissed him off, but instead he thought he could watch her in action all day. Now she was running back toward him in a sprint—and boy, could she run. Then the pain hit her again and she fell to the ground, moaning.

"Breathe," Arden whispered, trying to keep his voice low and calming.

"Brea...the? The pain is too much, you ass!"

Arden could listen to the woman's velvety voice all day, even if she was being mean. Before he could say anything else, she passed out. He couldn't help but smile at her. Her temper matched her hair that was for sure. And those green eyes were just as fiery. He was enthralled with her the moment he saw her. She was beautiful.

Arden picked her up and started carrying her back to his SUV. Bane and Tate shifted and started putting on what was left of their clothes.

"Their vehicle was parked at the edge of the woods. Someone was waiting for them, and they took off before we could get to them," Bane explained. "Is she okay?" he asked, eyeing Quinn, who was groaning in her sleep.

"She's already started the change. I need to get her back to the pack house. Bane, you go explain to Deaton about Finley. Tate will drive us back to the house so I can hold onto her. Then get him to drive you out to the house. I need to get her back before she wakes up." Arden continued carrying Quinn back to his vehicle without waiting for an answer.

"You got it, Alpha. Here's a purse, I bet it belongs to her." Bane picked it up and tossed it to Tate.

"Here, Alpha, let me hold her for you."

"No! I've got her." Arden had never felt such a possessive instinct for anyone in his life. He'd never had a woman make him want to just hold her and gaze at her beautiful face. He got in the back with her, but instead of laying her across the backseat, Arden held on to her as she snuggled up to him in her sleep. Even her scent was unbelievably appealing. He wanted to roll around in it and rub up against her until he couldn't smell anything but her.

"Alpha, you okay?" Tate asked. Arden pulled her body closer and sniffed her hair before he glanced up. "Your eyes have changed."

Arden closed his eyes. Her pheromones were unraveling him, and he knew that the woman in his arms was his mate. Her body's chemistry was already changing, even as he took in the different scents that made her so unique. She smelled like vanilla and coffee. He wanted to laugh. Apparently, his mate drank a lot of coffee with vanilla mixed in, and chocolate too.

"Do I smell vanilla?" Tate asked, scenting the air.

"She drinks a lot of coffee with vanilla and chocolate." Arden commented then pushed her hair behind her ears. "She's beautiful," he muttered.

When he glanced up, Tate was watching him in the rearview mirror. It didn't matter to him how crazy he sounded. This was his mate. He'd waited for her for a long, long time.

As he watched, her body started shaking in her sleep. The thought of the pain she'd have to endure to become a werewolf broke his heart. Quinn never asked for this, but she was still alive and that meant she was strong. The change was coming on fast. Arden held her closer, knowing that they didn't have much time left before she woke up, and when she did she would be pissed. It was the nature of the beast, and the fact that another wolf was holding her so close. The type of wolf she would be was still up in the air, but from what he'd just witnessed, she was an Alpha. She didn't cry or freak out when the wolf attacked her—no, his mate fought back and held her own. Arden figured she would try and fight him when she woke up, and in a way he was looking forward to it.

"Tell Rick to open up the other room and have it ready," Arden instructed Tate, who was already on the phone. The two rooms they were using to keep the newly turned wolves were usually small conference rooms where pack business was discussed.

The front gate was open, and Tate drove through. Rick opened the door for them when they arrived at the pack house so Arden could carry in Quinn. He could smell her wolf waking up inside her; he only had a few minutes before the fight was on. He ran up the stairs and inside the house.

Finley was standing at the door, watching, as Arden ran past him to the other room. He was a new wolf, and would quickly scent another wolf changing. He laid Quinn down on the bed just as her eyes popped open. They'd already turned yellow, and Arden backed up slowly. Before he made it more than one step, she was up in a crouched position.

"Do you remember me?" Arden asked calmly, being careful not to make any sudden movements. She nodded. "My name is Arden Dixon, and I know this may seem impossible to you, but a wolf bit you and your body is changing. You're changing into a werewolf."

He waited, letting that information sink in. She didn't make any noise until her nostrils flared and she scented the air. Arden knew what was coming when she caught his scent. Her eyes were switching back and forth from human to wolf, until those cold yellow eyes settled on him, where he stood blocking the door. Tate must have seen the look, too. He closed the door, locking Arden and Quinn together inside the room. As the door closed he could see in her eyes she was going to go for it. Like most young wolves, there wasn't much common sense in her train of thought. Survival was the only thing on her mind, and right now Arden was blocking her one escape route.

"I know you feel powerful right now, like you can take on the world, but you could really hurt someone, and I don't think you really want to hurt anyone. Especially me." Arden smiled, but Quinn didn't smile back. In fact, she started snarling. "I'm here to help you get through the change, and then we can talk about what comes next."

Arden knew what was going to happen when Quinn narrowed her eyes at him. She was getting ready to bolt, and if it took going through him she was sure going to give it one hell of a try. He could see that she was scared, but he didn't believe in sugar-coating what was going to happen. Plus, she was his mate, and he planned to keep her safe—even from herself.

"Quinn, take it easy, baby. Just take in some deep breaths." Quickly, Arden took his coat off and threw it to the ground before it could get ruined, then kicked his boots off. Quinn's eyes widened as Arden started stripping, and that was when the change struck. She shifted quickly, but her clothes were hung up around her legs, hindering her from charging Arden before he got to her. She needed to learn that he was the Alpha, and unfortunately she would learn it the hard way: by having his teeth sink into her throat.

His jaws wrapped around her neck as he pinned her to the floor. His mate was strong. She flailed around trying to free herself from his grip, but Arden held on and tried his best not to hurt her too badly. He could feel her sharp teeth digging into his leg as she tried to get him to let her go, but he'd been hurt worse. This was nothing. She didn't have any experience fighting as a wolf, which was a plus for him.

He could feel his teeth slicing further into her neck as he put more pressure on, and the taste of her blood flooded his mouth. If he'd had any doubts that she was his mate, he didn't now. All he wanted to do was fuck her hard.

Finally she realized that if she continued to jerk away from him he could rip her throat out. She gave up and went limp. He licked at her wounds, and with her new accelerated healing the bite marks closed quickly. The wolf had her eyes closed, trying to calm herself down. Only Alpha wolves could control themselves so readily.

He kept her pinned; to make sure she wasn't going to attack him again. Within a few minutes she shifted back to her human form. He shifted back as well, still covering her body. She was still breathing hard, but at least she was calm.

"Get off me." Her voice was still angry, and he didn't want to have to subdue her again. Reluctantly he slid off of her and sat back in a crouch, waiting. He watched as she glanced over her shoulder at him, and then crawled over to the couch. "I need some clothes."

He wanted to run his tongue all over her body. She was absolutely breathtaking. She was breathing hard as she continued trying to relax her body, and he couldn't help but stare at her large, stunning breasts. All he wanted to do was suck on them, then bite down on her shoulder and make her his forever. Before he had time to yell out to Tate to get her some clothes, the door opened and a bag was thrown inside. The door immediately slammed shut and locked again.

*****

Arden grabbed the bag and looked inside. "It's a t-shirt and sweatpants. Sorry, but you'll have to wait a bit to get undies." Arden laughed, but she wasn't amused. She rolled her eyes and leaned over to snatch the clothes from him.

Arden pulled them away before she could reach them. "Not so fast. I think we need to get something straight. First, I wasn't the one who bit you and turned you into a wolf, so you can quit being pissed at me. I'm only trying to help. Second, you can drop the bad-ass attitude, because right now you're in a situation where you need my help. I hold all the control. And third, you could at least say thank you."

All Quinn could focus on was the word 'control.' Her fingertips tingled, and she knew that if she called out inside for her wolf, claws would burst out. Nobody would ever control her again. Not this man, not her father, not anybody else who tried.

"Control?" Quinn laughed. "No man will ever control me. Now give me the clothes so I can leave."

"I'm sorry, but you can't leave," the man said. *What did he say his name was? Arden Dixon, that's it.* "Yeah, well Arden Dixon, you can't keep me here against my will. I don't care how much control you think you have."

Quinn watched as the man snorted, dropped the bag down in front of her, then picked up his clothes and walked to the door. The door opened for him then immediately closed again. She could hear the lock click, and that was when she lost her temper. She ran as fast as she could, ramming the door with her shoulder, but it didn't even budge. Her shoulder didn't hurt either, which surprised her.

"Let me out!" she screamed, but nobody responded.

*****

Arden and Tate were walking off when they heard Quinn's body slam against the door. Both of them jerked around as the woman screamed out.

"Shit. Did you hear how hard she hit that door?" Tate asked, but Arden was too busy glaring at it. "Good thing we got those doors reinforced."

Arden turned back around again, ready to walk out, when Finley stopped him. "What's going on, Alpha?"

Arden moved closer to Finley's door. "Another person was bitten, and she's a little pissed off."

"Yeah, I can hear that. She doesn't like you much," Finley said, then moved away from the window.

Arden didn't know why, but the statement hurt him for some reason. Quinn was his mate, and he wanted her to feel about him the way he was starting to feel about her. It was too soon for anything as powerful as love, but he'd accept not getting his head ripped off. Because if her anger toward him was as bad as the hit to the door indicated, he was in bad shape.

Arden was sitting down at the kitchen table with his head in his hands when Alice walked in and rubbed her hand down his back. "Hey there, lover."

This was something—someone—he didn't want to deal with right now. "I'm not in the mood, Alice."

"I bet I can get you in the mood, Alpha." Alice's voice grated on his nerves. She pushed her fingers through his hair, letting her nails scratch against his scalp. She did know how he liked it, but now he'd met his mate, and her touch produced no reaction except irritation.

"Alice, stop!" Arden pushed her hands away just as Tate walked in with an envelope in his hands.

"Leave, Alice." Tate gave her a firm stare. She started to walk off, but not before rolling her eyes at him. Once she was gone, Tate handed the official-looking envelope to Arden.

"What is this?" Arden asked, then turned it over and saw the seal. It was from the Council, and Arden knew what was in it before he even opened it.

He broke the seal, read the note, and put it back in the envelope.

"What did they say?" Tate sat down across from him.

"They're sending a few Death Hunters to help with the search for the rogue pack. 'Before it gets out of hand,' they said."

"Fucking Death Hunters? Damn, they'll just come in and kill everybody, innocents included," Tate raged.

"Tate, I need you to calm down. If we panic, the pack will pick that emotion up and they'll be scared too. We can't allow them to see that we're upset. We have to find this pack before it's too late and the Council sends a whole squad. Right now it looks like they're only sending two. When they get here, put them on the other side of the house from the pack."

"That's where we stay, Alpha."

"I know that, and I want them close to us. I want to know what they're doing at all times. Understood?" Arden put his hand on Tate's shoulder, sending soothing emotions through their bond. He needed for Tate to cool down and understand that they were still in charge.

Tate closed his eyes and inhaled deeply. "You got it, Alpha."

"Now you go take care of making sure that the rooms are ready for them when they get here, and I'll go check on Quinn to see if she has calmed down."

Arden put on the rest of his clothes, but before he went back to Quinn's room, he remembered something and ran off to the kitchen. "Where do they keep it?"

"Keep what, Alpha?" Jade Cross asked. Arden smiled at Bane's little sister, although she wasn't so little anymore. She was a beautiful lady who he'd watched grow up and considered a sister himself.

"Hey there, Squirt."

"You do realize I'm an adult now?" Jade asked with a smile. The thin scar across her check only added character, he thought. She was still beautiful.

"Of course, but to me you'll always be a squirt." Arden kissed her on the head and started pulling open cabinet doors.

"What are you looking for?" Jade asked, still smiling.

"I want to make Quinn some coffee with some vanilla and chocolate in it. You think you can help an old man out?"

"For one, you're not old, and yes I can." Jade started pulling ingredients out of the pantry. He chuckled as she pointed to the items, then started making it for him. While she was busy he took a good look at Jade and found that she'd grown up. He still remembered the bear getting a hold of her when she was just a pup. They hadn't known if she would live, but she was full of fight. She'd survived, but every time she looked in a mirror she would always remember that experience.

"Can I do anything else for you, Alpha?" Jade held the cup up for him. It smelled just like his mate.

He smiled, "Yes, you can." Arden explained what he needed Jade to do, and then left to bring the coffee to his mate.

As he passed by Finley's door, he looked in the window and saw Finley was doing push-ups. Then he peered through Quinn's door and found his mate unscrewing the screens from the vents. He wanted to laugh, but he didn't want her to be even more furious with him.

He turned the lock and opened the door. "I don't think you'll fit through those vents."

She continued to work without turning around.

"I brought you some coffee."

"You can't keep me here, Arden." Quinn continued unscrewing the vent, with what looked like a butter knife.

He needed to make sure the rooms were cleaned more thoroughly if any more humans were bitten. Someone must've eaten in here and left their utensils.

"Sure I can." Arden couldn't help but prod her some. He put the coffee down on the counter beside her, and she looked over at it and narrowed her eyes.

"Does that have vanilla and chocolate in it?"

"Yes. I could smell it on you earlier and I figured you drank it a lot."

*****

Damn, the man was being nice. But why? She took a good look at her capturer. He was handsome, that was for sure. In fact, she would go so far as to say he was downright gorgeous, with his black hair that needed a trim and the five o'clock shadow covering his jaw. Man, would she like to… Damn, she needed to stop looking at him. He was keeping her here against her will, but he did bring her favorite coffee. "Thanks, that was thoughtful of you, but you can't control me with coffee." Quinn closed her eyes as a memory of her father flashed into her mind.

"Father, you can't take my doll away from me. I paid for it with my own money."

"Sure I can."

She's hated her father because he wouldn't ever give the doll back to her. He kept it to prove to her that he held all the power. After that day, she never purchased anything she loved too much to lose. She opened up a bank account in another town and never told anyone how much money she had in it, so that when she ran away she would have some start-up money. And now this asshole thought he was going to control her? She would never let that happen again, no matter how nice he was being.

Putting her face in her hands, she dropped to the floor. "You're just like him."

Arden rushed to her side. "What's wrong?"

"Get away from me! I want out of here. I have a store to get ready to run. People will know I'm missing. My family will cause all kinds of trouble if you don't let me out."

"Quinn, I'm not trying to hold you hostage. I want you to understand that you just turned into a wolf, dammit. Don't you get it? Life has changed for you, woman." She could see the frustration in his face as he spoke.

"I understand that, but telling me that I'm not ever leaving isn't helping me! I have a lot to do before the store opens this weekend,"

Quinn answered. The man just didn't get it. "Look, I understand, and I want to learn how to deal with this. But right now, all I can think about is my future, and that's making Southern Treasures a success."

"You changed the name of the store?" Arden sat down on the couch.

She raised her chin. "Yes, among other things." Arden didn't speak, but seemed to be waiting expectantly. "Do you want to know what I've changed?"

"Yes, I do," he said, actually looking interested.

Quinn narrowed her eyes, but walked around the chair and sat down. "Well, for starters, I painted the inside of the shop and put up new counters and pictures. Then I put up my collection of clothes and shoes. I also put in a jewelry counter with a lot of pieces from local artists. If all goes to plan, the store should bring in a lot of business for the community, like the diner and the art gallery. Maybe other stores will open up, too." She crossed her arms and waited for Arden's response.

"Do you have clothes for me, too?" Arden asked with smirk.

"Yes, I do, but I'm still getting in some more stock for the men's collection. That's why I need to get back to the store and unload the shipments that I know have come in by now," Quinn pointed out.

"Maybe in a few days we can help you with that." Arden knew a fight was coming now. He wanted her close, and if she went back to the store she would be away from him, and in danger. The rogue pack was still on the loose, and he couldn't chance her getting hurt. The mating pull was playing havoc on him every time he inhaled her unique scent of vanilla and chocolate.

"A few days? I can't wait a few... Why?" Quinn sputtered.

"For one, you're in danger of being abducted by the pack that bit you. We have a rogue pack going around biting humans, and that is unacceptable."

"That's your problem, not mine. I'm a victim, not a prisoner. I did nothing wrong but go outside to get my purse," she argued.

He had to tell her what she meant to him. She needed to know the truth.

"I have to be honest with you, Quinn. Do you know what a mate is to werewolves?"

"Mate, like—" Quinn stopped talking and thought for a minute. "You mean like a friend or something?"

"Yeah, something like that." Arden scratched his head. "To a wolf a mate is more than a friend. A mate is who we're fated to be with forever. I'll never want another person, love another person, or hell, have sex with anyone but you."

Quinn jumped up and circled behind the couch, putting it between them. "Oh no you don't. I'm not going to be your love slave or something like that. You let me go *now.*"

"Stop, and calm down. You're not listening to me." Arden put his hands up, trying to placate her.

"What are you leaving out, the part where you tie me up and then have your way with me?" Quinn was panicking now. She picked up a throw pillow and held it in front of her like a shield. "Look, I may have been bitten by a werewolf, but that doesn't give you the right to make me have sex with you."

"You're right, and I'm not trying to force you to do anything. But I want you to at least talk to someone beside me about it. Maybe they can explain it better—" Arden inhaled "—because right now all I want to do is fuck you." He got up to leave, needing to get away from her scent, then stopped and leaned his head against the door. "Quinn, I'm sorry. I didn't mean for this to happen. I know you're my mate, but you need someone who can explain this to you besides me. I've got to get out of here." Arden could smell her excitement, even though she was scared too, and it was tearing him up. He opened the door and walked out before he did something he would regret later.

He leaned against the wall outside and panted, thinking about how close he just came in jumping her, ripping her clothes off, and having his way with her. Then she had to mention him tying her up, and that was it—he had to leave, or he was sure to do it.

Jade was coming around the corner with a tray of food.

"Great timing. Jade, I need your help."

"Of course Alpha." She sat the tray down on a side table.

"I need you to talk to Quinn and explain what an Alpha's mate is. She's my mate, Jade, and she doesn't understand what that means. I can't stay in the room long enough to really talk to her about it, or I'm…"

"Oh, okay. Sure, I can do it." Jade smiled, and then blushed.

"Thank you, Jade." Arden kissed the top of Jade's head and then walked away, because right now the further he got away from Quinn, the better.

Chapter 4

Quinn heard someone whispering through the air vent and went to sit down next to it.

"Hellooo." She giggled, because whoever was speaking tried to say it like a little kid would talk into a fan.

She leaned in closer. "Hello back to you."

"I feel like I'm a prisoner in a movie and I find out that someone else is being kept next door."

Quinn's eyes widened as the voice spoke. "No, you're not alone. Wait; this a joke?" Quinn asked. If it were then she would just go flop on the couch, or maybe run laps around the room because that's what she wanted to do anyway.

"No, I'm in here too. I've been bitten as well. Arden said you were bitten soon after me."

Quinn leaned in closer as the voice stopped talking. "Really? What's your name?"

"Finley Egan. What's your name?"

"Quinn Lamone."

"Well, Quinn, it's nice to meet you."

"You too, Finley. Hey wait, someone's coming." Quinn got up and stood behind the couch. The door was unlocked, and a young lady with blonde hair walked in. Quinn took a step back when the woman looked up, revealing the scar that stretched across her face.

"Hi," the young woman said hesitantly.

"Hey." Quinn tried not to stare, but she couldn't stop herself. "Did...did they do that to your face?" Quinn knew the moment she said it that it was a stupid question to ask, but apparently she was a glutton for punishment.

"No! Of course not. Why would you ask something like that? Have they been mean to you, or showed you anything but kindness since you got here?" Jade demanded.

Her scar stood out more when she frowned. "I'm sorry, I shouldn't have asked that. It was rude and inconsiderate of me. I do apologize for my insulting behavior, but I'm a little stressed out here. First, I've been bitten by a wolf and told, 'oh yeah, now you're a werewolf.' Then the big, good-looking guy tells me I'm his mate and all he wants to do is have sex with me. Then he tells me I can't leave. Yep, I'm a little pissed off right now, so please excuse my rudeness." Quinn walked around the couch and stuck her hand out to the woman.

"My name is Quinn Lamone. I just moved to town and opened up a new store called Southern Treasures, and now I'm a werewolf."

"Really, you the one who bought Charlotte's Closet? This is great. Now we'll have someplace to go and buy our books," Jade said happily.

"Unfortunately, I don't have any books right now. It's a clothing store, with jewelry and other things, but no books. Sorry." Quinn sat down on the couch across from Jade.

Jade shrugged. "I always thought that Charlotte should've had a small book section with coffeemakers on the side and places for men to sit while their wives shopped, but Charlotte never wanted to do it. I just thought it would look pretty cool."

"I've never thought about it, but I'll look into it. I do have other things that you may like," Quinn assured her. "Jewelry and purses, stuff like that."

"Purses? I love purses."

"Then you need to come check the store out! I have all kinds. I was hoping to sell some of Janice Evans' purses. But she turned me down, saying the store wasn't big enough and the town was too small." Quinn looked over at the small purse Jade had draped over her shoulder. "I love your purse, actually. Who made it?"

Jade laughed, then pulled it off and showed it to her. "I made this."

Quinn couldn't believe she'd made the purse herself. The quality was excellent, and the vibrant colors were the coolest she'd ever seen. "You made this?"

Jade nodded.

"Wow, Jade. This is wonderful, and gorgeous. You should sell these. I mean, have you ever sold any?"

"No. I usually give them away for presents, but everyone seems to love them," Jade said.

"Girl, I could get at least fifty dollars for these small ones with my online store, and even sell them in the shop. I use a lot of local artists and people who don't sell through mainstream channels. Would you be interested? You'd need to get a stockpile, with examples for me to put on the site, and then extras in case they sell. Well, I *know* they'd sell."

"Oh, I have lots made already. I just put them in boxes when I'm finished making them. Here, let me show you what I have." Jade pulled out her phone and opened up her pictures. She handed the phone to Quinn, who sat there and looked at picture after picture of the coolest purses she'd ever seen.

"Jade, these are wonderful. I mean the quality is first-rate, and the colors go so well together. They're so cool. You have to let me sell these for you."

A new smile graced Jade's face at her announcement. "Yeah, I guess. Are you sure?"

"Yes I'm sure. You'll make a fortune. Now we need to put these pictures on my website to sell. Do you have a laptop?"

"Yes, hold on. I'll be right back." Jade started to leave the room, then turned abruptly and sat back down. "I forgot to tell you something. You mentioned mates, and I don't think you actually get what a mate means to my kind. You see, we wait our whole lives to meet our mate. We get one mate in a lifetime, and that person fits us perfectly. That person will love us and we will only mate with that one person forever. We don't cheat, or even have the urge to cheat. I know humans sometimes get divorced and move on to someone else, but not us. We never want to leave our mate. Sure, we get mad at each other, but we never get the urge to leave. It's a way of ensuring the continuation of our race and to keep us going. Arden, our Alpha, says you're his mate. I figure since you've just been changed it may take a while before that mating pull gets a hold of you, but don't you worry; once it does, girl, all you'll want to do is have…well, lots of sex." Jade whispered the last part bashfully. "Now, let me go get the laptop." She got up, leaving Quinn alone with this new information.

*****

Jade locked the door behind her, but before she could head to her room, she saw Alice leaning against the wall.

"What're you up to, Scarface?" Alice giggled at her own joke.

"Nothing." Jade tried to brush past, but Alice jumped in front of her.

"Nothing? It didn't look like nothing to me. Looked like you were trying to make a friend, Scarface. But nobody wants to be your friend. They'd get sick to their stomach looking at your big fat scar all the time." Alice reached out and traced the scar with her finger.

Jade could feel the tears coming, and she tried again to get away, but Alice grabbed her and punched her in the stomach. Jade gasped as she fell to her knees.

"Just remember, nobody wants to be your friend, even the new girl," Alice told her, then sauntered off like she didn't have a care in the world.

Jade let her tears fall until she heard a voice say, "You should stick up for yourself." It was the new wolf, Finley.

She couldn't face him right now; she was too embarrassed. Looking away, Jade ran off to her room.

*****

"Dammit." Unfortunately, Jade had locked the door when she left, but she did leave her phone. Not wasting another minute, Quinn dialed 911 and waited for the operator to answer.

"Hello, New Hope Police Department. How can I help you?" *Good grief, they don't even have a 911 operator, it goes directly into the police department.*

"Hello, my name is Quinn Lamone, and I'm being held against my will at Arden…"

"Arden Dixon's house, ma'am? Is that where you're at?" the operator asked. Hell, everyone seemed to know the man.

"Yes, that's it. Please send someone to help me. Please." Quinn tried to sound desperate, but Jade was right; they were being nice to her. She looked over at the food the woman had brought: a big hamburger with french fries. It looked yummy.

"Honey, I've known Arden Dixon for a long time, and he wouldn't hurt a fly, much less a lady. I'll tell the chief, and you can talk to him." Then the lady hung up. Shit, she was in a crossover between *The Twilight Zone* and the freaking *Andy Griffith Show*. But that hamburger smelled good, and she was starving. Putting the phone down, Quinn reached over and practically inhaled the food.

Just as she was finishing, Jade ran back into the room with her laptop and a handful of purses. "I thought before you put them up for sale on your site, you should see the finished products." She dropped the purses into Quinn's lap, then sat down and opened her computer.

"These are wonderful, Jade. The work you've done on them is better than I've seen in a long time. Where did you find the fabric?" Quinn asked. Then she looked up at Jade and saw that her face was red, like she'd been crying.

"I dyed it myself. I find the colors that I want, and dye the material twice. Then it takes a few hours to sew it. I'm so used to it now that I keep getting faster, but it relaxes me and I love creating things." Jade looked over at her, but kept the scarred side of her face turned away.

"Are you okay?" Quinn asked, concerned.

"Yeah. What do you think of them?"

Letting it go, Quinn concentrated on the purses. "These are works of art, Jade. They're just extraordinary! Now let's find a place to hang them and then take some pictures." Quinn looked around the room and found a table sitting against the wall. She grabbed one of the purses and started setting them up. "We need a card that we can fold over and put the name of the purse on. Hmm, what should we call this one?"

"Rainbow Delight," Jade suggested.

Quinn's eyes widened. "Yes, yes, that's it. Rainbow Delight." She went over to a drawer she'd seen earlier and found a bunch of markers and construction paper. She cut out some name cards, and then drew a rainbow on one. Underneath it, she wrote, 'Rainbow Delight, by Jade Cross.' Then she took a picture with Jade's phone.

They named all the purses and took pictures of them with their tags. It didn't take long before Quinn had Jade Cross purses up on her website. She'd price some of them at fifty dollars, but the bigger ones would cost around a hundred and ten dollars.

"We never talked about my cut. Would ten percent of the sale be okay?" It wasn't hard putting the purses up on her site, and it wasn't really costing her much. If they did sell, and she knew they would, she'd come out with at least five percent in profit. "When they start to sell, we'll need to do some marketing for you, and then we can renegotiate the percentage." It was a win-win for them both.

"Sounds good to me." Jade and Quinn both laughed.

"Look you've already sold one." Quinn showed Jade. "You might want to go and start working on more stock. I've got a feeling you're going to need it," she suggested. She watched as the excited young woman stood up, then turned around so Quinn couldn't see her face.

"Jade, are you okay?" Quinn put her hand on her shoulder and turned her around to find that tears were falling down Jade's face. "What's the matter, Jade? Did I do something wrong?"

"No." Jade sniffled, wiping the tears from her face. "Nobody has ever done anything like this for me."

"What, been nice to you?" Quinn asked, shocked that nobody had showed this woman any kindness. Now she really wanted out of here.

"Yes. I only really have four friends, and that's because there's something wrong with each of us, so we stick together."

"What's wrong with you?" Quinn asked. She didn't think there was anything wrong with Jade.

"Isn't it obvious?" Jade pointed at the scar on her face.

"You have to be kidding me. You think something's wrong with you because of a scar on your face?"

"Well, yeah," Jade said hesitantly.

Quinn put her hand over her heart. "Jade, don't you ever let anyone tell you that you're not good enough because of a scar. Those bitches are probably just mean, spiteful people…. Damn, is Arden mean to you too?"

"Oh no, no, no. He would never do anything like that. Just some of the girls around here are a little mean, but that's okay because I don't want to be in their group anyway." Jade started picking up her purses and putting them in a bag.

"Jade, I hope we can be friends. Nothing is wrong with you, and whoever says different is an idiot." Quinn smiled, but Jade started laughing.

"I like you, Quinn, and yes, I hope we can be friends," Jade answered.

"Good." Quinn started scratching her arm. She rolled her shoulders, thinking she must need to take a shower, because she was feeling itchy all over.

"What's wrong?" Jade looked down at the arm she was scratching feverishly.

"I feel funny and I'm itchy all over." Quinn started pacing back and forth from the couch to the other end of the room.

"You need to release your wolf."

"What?"

"You need to shift, Quinn. Your wolf wants out, and you need to let her run. When you don't, you start to feel itchy and aggressive, like you could hit something."

"Yes, that's it," Quinn agreed with a huff.

"I'll go talk to the Alpha about getting you out of here." Jade went out, but locked the door behind her again.

"You're feeling it too?" she heard Finley ask from the other room.

Quinn walked back over to the air vent and crouched down. "Yes, are you?"

"I'm about to take the door down if they don't hurry up and let me out," he said. "Okay, someone's coming to my door. I'll let you know what's up in a minute."

Quinn stayed by the vent. She could hear someone opening up Finley's door. "Dad!"

"Son, are you alright?" Quinn could hear another voice. She knew she needed to get out of here, and she wasn't waiting on Arden to come back. Shit, as far as she could tell it looked he was going to keep her in here forever.

"Hello, can you hear me? Finley, are you in there?" Quinn yelled into the vent.

"Yes, Quinn, I'm here and so is my dad. He's the police chief."

"I'm being kept against my will. Please let me out, sir. I've done nothing wrong. I called my family and left a message on their phone that Arden Dixon was holding me captive. Please let me out." The last part was a lie, but she was itching all over. If he didn't let her go her wolf was going to tear the damn place down.

"Miss, I'll be in there to get you in a minute," the chief said.

"Hurry." Quinn was feeling desperate. Her breathing was changing, and apparently they could hear the difference. She could hear Finley tell his dad to go get help.

She laid down on the floor and closed her eyes to the sound of her clothes tearing apart as she shifted.

******

Arden could hear Bane yelling for him to come quick. All he could think was something had happened to Quinn. He rushed inside the hallway and found Deaton Egan, Bane, and Finley standing outside Quinn's room.

"What's happened?" He rushed over to look inside, and gasped. Quinn had shifted, and her wolf was tearing up the furniture and anything that she could get her jaws around. In fact, he wouldn't be surprised if she'd pissed all over everything. She looked that angry.

"Alpha, I think I'd let her calm down before I went in there," Deaton suggested.

"She needs to run. She told me she'd started itching and feeling funny. I've been looking for you. I take it she already shifted?" Jade asked as she walked up and glanced in the window.

"And tore the whole room apart." Bane laughed.

"It's not funny. You shut us up in this little room and expect us to just sit here, after you tell us that everything about our lives has changed. Yeah, I think she has a right to be pissed off," Finley said angrily.

Arden didn't know exactly how to take Finley standing up for Quinn, but he had a pissed-off female and he had to deal with that first. As soon as he opened the door, Quinn ran up and bit him on the hand. While he was still surprised, she slipped past him, out of the room. The bite didn't hurt; he figured it was a way for her to get some of her frustration out. He didn't take it to heart, he was reading her background and got carried away trying to find out about Quinn.

She zigzagged around the furniture in the living room. Seeing some of the pack members watching TV, she wheeled around and ran down another hallway, which led to the kitchen. He thought he might have her cornered, until her eyes flicked to the right and she saw the doggie door. *Damn, she's closer to it than I am.*

Arden could hear her nails trying to get some traction, but before he could catch her the kitchen door opened and Alice walked in. Quinn immediately charged past her and took off into the woods. She was fast. Shifting, Arden ran after her. He knew that Bane and the others were following too, but he needed to be the one who caught his mate. The best way to do that was to alert the pack and have her turned back into his direction. Stopping, he howled into the sky telling his pack to run her back toward the house.

He trotted back to the house and shifted back into his human form. Bane, Finley, Deaton, and Alice were all waiting for him. Alice threw him a set of sweatpants, and he put them on. He could tell that Finley wanted to run, but he patiently waited next to his dad anyway.

He could hear his pack howling to each other as they herded her in the direction of the pack house. He smiled as she ran out of the woods and skittered to a stop. She was mad, but also tired from all the running. She wasn't used to it, and that was something she needed to work on. Her wolf would want to run a lot.

He bent down and got on her eye level. The whole pack came out of the woods to watch the Alpha address their newest pack member.

"Quinn, shift now," Arden ordered. When she didn't obey, he shifted to his wolf form and growled at her. All Alphas had an innate ability to intimidate. Most used it when fighting, but sometimes they had to use it to get one of their wolves under control. When she didn't obey, Arden's growl got downright vicious, until Quinn dropped to the ground in fear.

"Stop, you're scaring her!" Finley started to intervene, but Deaton stopped him.

"This is the way it is, son. He's the Alpha, and you have to trust that he knows what he's doing."

"Shift, Quinn!" Finley yelled. "He'll stop if you shift."

But nothing worked. Quinn got up, and this time Arden got so close his powerful jaws grazed her. She shifted back to human and curled up in a ball. "I want to go home."

Alice snorted, and Bane looked over at her. Jade ran up and handed Quinn some clothes, then stood in front of her while she slipped them on. When she was dressed, Quinn stood and walked up to Deaton.

"I want to go home, *now*."

"Okay," Deaton muttered reluctantly.

"She can't go home; she's in danger from the pack that changed her," Arden interrupted. He'd shifted back while Quinn was getting dressed.

"I don't care, Chief. I'm not his prisoner. I have a right to go home."

"You can't keep her here, Arden. It's her choice. And if my son wants to leave, he can too," Deaton told him.

"Then she goes with guards. The rogue pack wanted her—they won't stop until they get her, and I'm not going to let that happen." Arden replied. He was pissed but Quinn didn't care. The man just hit her with some kind of voodoo vibes of his and she wasn't going to be any one's bitch again.

Arden felt like the ground had just dropped out from under his feet. The sense of abandonment he'd felt at his parents' deaths flooded back to him. *What if something happened to her too?* Thinking about something happening to her now that he'd just found her shook him to the core.

"Okay, until we find this pack then she has guards," Deaton agreed, looking at Quinn. "This isn't optional, Quinn. We don't know exactly who we're dealing with here, and more people have disappeared in two towns nearby. These people are dangerous."

He could see his mate thinking about it. He knew she didn't like the thought of having guards, but she was going to have to accept it.

"Okay, but I have to get my store ready for the grand opening," Quinn muttered.

Thank God she'd agreed. If she only knew how hard this was for him. She'd just been turned, so who could say when the mating pull would start with her. It was already eating him up inside. Now he would be worried sick about her safety. "Tate, Rod, Morris, and Jake you're on guard detail. Finley, what are you going to do?" Arden asked.

"I plan to help Quinn get her store up and running, but I'll come back here at night if that's okay?" Finley answered. Even his dad looked shocked that he was choosing to stay at the pack house.

He needed to find out what Finley was up to. Quinn was his mate, and no matter what he wasn't giving Finley a shot at her. "Finley, before you leave I need to talk to you for a minute." Arden walked back into the house as everyone, including Quinn, stared after him.

He stood by the kitchen counter, waiting until Finley walked inside. "What is your deal when it comes to Quinn?" Finley actually looked surprised, which was good for him. Because if he wanted to be anything other than friends with her, Arden would have to rip his head off. Just thinking of him touching her was driving him crazy.

"We have a lot in common, and I hope we're friends," Finley answered.

"Just so you know, she's my mate," Arden told him.

"Yeah, I heard you tell her that, and Jade explained it. I don't think she's interested right now, but lucky for you we're just friends." Finley said smugly.

Arden grabbed Finley around the neck and slammed him against the wall. "Remember who you're talking to, boy. I understand that you're an Alpha, but I'm *your* Alpha and you damn well need to fucking remember that. Are we clear?" Arden wasn't really hurting Finley, but hopefully it got his point across.

"Yes, Alpha. I got it," Finley said, still smiling. Arden could tell he was just trying to appease him. "I'm not interested in her like that," he repeated, then walked out the door.

Arden could tell that before this was all over they were going to fight, and he would have to show the kid who was boss. Right now, though, his mate was mad at him—and she was leaving.

Chapter 5

Quinn got in the back of the squad car with Finley. Deaton was taking her back to her small apartment above the store, and right now all she could think about was taking a shower and going to bed. She had a big day ahead of her tomorrow and she needed all the rest she could get.

There wasn't any conversation in the car. When the chief pulled up at the store, a truckload of wolves pulled up right behind them. She got out, and Bane came up to her. "We'll change shifts every six hours. My orders are to make sure everything is okay before you go inside. I need to check out your apartment, just to make sure nobody's broken in."

Quinn reached into her purse and took out her keys, and then they all went around to the back of the store and up the stairs. Bane asked them to wait at the door and went in first. He turned on all the lights, but she could actually see in the dark, so she knew he could too. If there was a plus in being turned it was definitely the night vision; that had to be the coolest trick. Now she could save a fortune on electricity at night.

"Everything looks good in here. You can come in." They entered her apartment behind her and looked around. When she dropped her purse on the table and turned, all the wolves were standing by a picture on the wall. "Did you draw this?" Bane asked.

"Yeah, I've always loved wolves. One day that image just came to me, and I drew it. Guess it's kinda ironic." Quinn snorted.

Finley walked over and looked at it. "You're good, too."

"Thanks. I love to draw. Guess now I can see wolves up close and personal."

Finley laughed. "I guess so. If they're all watching over you tonight then I'm going to my dad's to get my clothes, and then I'll head back to the pack house. If you need some help, I don't have a job right now, so I can help you do some repairs or build stuff for the store tomorrow. I need something to keep my mind off...well, this."

"I can pay you for your help. I'll be downstairs around eight tomorrow. I have a lot to do, and I could really use a hand," Quinn answered.

"Well, I won't turn down getting paid." Finley laughed, and then looked at his dad. "You ready, Pop?"

"Yep. Quinn, here's my card. If you need me, please call my cell phone. I don't live far from here, but I don't think I'll have to worry too much about you tonight. Good night." Deaton Egan smiled and walked out.

She liked Finley's dad. He had some grey in his hair, but otherwise he looked just like his son. Finley had close-cropped brown hair and hazel eyes. He was a cutie, and she was really glad to have him as a friend. She felt that she could say anything to him and he wouldn't tell a soul. The girls would go crazy over his good looks and confident nature, but what she liked best about him was that he didn't seem arrogant about his looks. She got the feeling that Deaton was the same way.

"Bye Quinn. See you in the morning." Finley left behind his dad.

Quinn waved good-bye to them. Now all she wanted was to take a hot bath, and if these wolves thought they were staying here, they were crazy. "You're not staying in my apartment, Bane."

"I know," he said.

"I understand that I need protection, and you can either stay in the store or outside, but not in my apartment."

"Okay. I'll keep your keys so I can get inside the store, and we'll keep one guard at your door and one in front of the store. Scream if you need anything," Bane said with a wink, and then they left.

Quinn locked the door and went to run herself a tub full of hot water. She was tired and desperate to just relax.

Sitting down in the steaming water, Quinn wanted to moan, but she was afraid the guard outside would think she was in trouble. She didn't need a bunch of wolves breaking her door in. Leaning back, she wondered how her life had come to this.

What in the hell happened today? It was just her luck that a damn wolf would pick her to bite.

Arden Dixon's face continued to plague her thoughts, and it was starting to piss her off. The man was an egotistical control freak, just like her father, and she couldn't be with anyone who thought they were going to run her life. However, Quinn couldn't deny her immediate desire for his gorgeous body. How on earth could she be attracted to him when he tried to tell her what to do every minute of the day?

Quinn lathered soap on her skin, and noticed that her body had changed since she was bitten. Closing her eyes, she felt her muscles, and could tell that she was more defined and toned now. Well, that was a plus, because she'd thought she was getting fat. When she felt her stomach, she found it was flat and smooth now. That was definitely something to feel good about.

Then she remembered she could see in the dark now, too. She had so many questions to ask Jade tomorrow. What else would she be able to do besides changing into a wolf? Would she be a superhero now? Quinn laughed at herself. She had a lot to think about, including what she would do about Arden.

Arden.

Her thoughts drifted back to him again. As Quinn touched her stomach, she imagined it was his hand drifting upward to her breasts. She could feel her nipples harden just at the thought of him touching her there. Pinching herself harder, she rubbed her hand down and touched herself between the legs. It felt wonderful. The warm water felt soothing as she rubbed her finger over her clit. It wouldn't take long, as she fantasized about Arden touching her faster and faster until he plunged his long finger inside of her.

Quinn didn't have time to prepare—she went off like a firecracker inside the tub, splashing water over the side and soaking the floor, but she didn't care. She smiled at the thought of Arden touching her. He was the best fantasy she'd ever had.

As her body calmed down, Quinn almost fell asleep in the water. Feeling dead on her feet, Quinn decided to worry about everything that was going on later. Right now she was going to go to bed. She got out of the tub reluctantly and dried off, then slipped under the covers and fell asleep.

*****

Arden slipped through the woods in his wolf form, then sat at the edge of the trees, watching the light go off in the upstairs apartment. He needed to be near Quinn and make sure she was going to be okay. Jade said that Quinn wasn't the type of person to follow the rules; she wanted to be an independent person, and that meant she needed time to get used to this type of life, a pack life. Members of a pack were always in each other's business. He needed to understand that and give her some space, but Arden was an Alpha, and he didn't know if he could keep his distance from his mate. He was going to try, though, because he wanted her happy.

"I figured you'd show up soon." Bane sat down on the ground beside him.

"Scent anything?" Arden asked, shifting back.

"Nothing. The smell is gone, and there isn't anything new," Bane said. They sat in silence for a few minutes before Bane spoke again. "Your mate is an artist. When I checked her apartment out I saw a picture on the wall that she drew, of wolves standing around watching the moon come up. It was real cool."

"Bite of the Moon. Maybe she'll let me see it one day," Arden joked.

"What do you mean by 'Bite of the Moon?'" Bane asked.

"She was turned by the Bite of the Moon. Old tales that say that those who are bitten on the day of a full moon will be powerful wolves."

"Hmm. So, you were born on a full moon, right?"

"Yep," Arden answered absently, staring up at her window.

"Makes sense, then. Oh yeah, before I forget: Finley's going home to get his things, and then he's headed back to the pack house."

"What do you think of him?" Arden asked.

"I like the kid. I think in time he'll make a great guard. He's smart, and he'd be an asset to us. We just need to teach him who the Alpha is." Bane laughed.

"I think that's going to happen sooner rather than later." Arden glanced back up at Quinn's apartment.

"How do you think she'll adjust to pack life?" Bane asked.

"I don't know. I want her to want to be with us, but right now I can't force her, or she'll hate me for it. I just need to keep her alive if the rogues find her again. I can't take a chance of anyone getting to her. I think it would—"

"Kill you. I understand that you want your mate safe, I think we all get that, but you can be a tad controlling." Bane held his fingers up, an inch apart.

"When you find your mate, Bane, you'll feel the same way."

"Well, she's asleep, and you need to go and get rest some too. She'll be here tomorrow. We get relieved in the morning, and you can come check on her then. But go get some sleep while you can," Bane suggested. "I've got a feeling we're all going to need it."

"You trying to tell me what to do, Beta?" Arden asked.

Bane raised his eyebrow. "If I need to, Alpha."

"See you tomorrow. Be safe." Arden shifted and ran back into the woods. Bane was right; he needed some rest. Tomorrow was going to be a long day.

Chapter 6

Quinn woke up early the next morning, took a quick shower, and got dressed. She couldn't get over how wonderful she felt. She laughed to herself as she looked in the mirror. Her skin had never looked better, and her red hair, which she'd always hated, was shiny and soft. It had to be the changes taking place in her body. She felt ready to take on the world.

Grabbing her jacket, Quinn opened the door and saw Bane leaning up against the stair railing. "Brought you a donut and some coffee. Arden said to make sure you had vanilla and chocolate in it."

"Wow, can I expect this type of treatment every day? If so, I think I'm going to like being a wolf." Quinn reached over and took the coffee and bag of donuts, then kissed Bane on the cheek.

"Thank your mate; he was the one who thought of it. I was hungry, too, and you need to feed your wolf or she'll get cranky. I really don't want to put my people through your wrath because you're not eating enough. Remember to have a snack about every two hours; we have to feed often." Bane moved so she could walk down the stairs first.

"Thanks for being so nice to me, Bane. I know I was a real bitch yesterday, but I…"

"Don't worry about it. I think I would have been the same way. It's a lot to take in. Maybe getting the store ready will help relieve some of your stress. Finley's already here, and we have wolves both outside and inside the store, keeping an eye out for the rogues. I'll be back later this evening. Should I bring you something to eat?"

"Probably." Quinn giggled.

Bane opened the back door to the store and let her in. "Hey, lock this behind you, and I'll see you in a few."

"Okay. Thanks again." Quinn locked the door and walked through to the sales floor, where she found Finley, Jade, and three other people she didn't know.

"Hey, Quinn. I brought my purses, and the boxes I already had to put them in. Last night I looked online and found some good ones and had my logo put on them. What do you think?" Jade held up her laptop and showed Quinn the pictures she'd saved. "They should be here in a couple of days."

Quinn glanced at the boxes and smiled. "You have a great eye for this, Jade. I can't wait to see what you come up with next."

"Well, I make jewelry too," Jade added.

"You're kidding." Quinn's eyes sparked with interest. "Well, come look at the counter I had made for the jewelry. I think I can get another counter built and add yours to it. Hey Fin, can you build a counter like that one?" She pointed.

"Sure can. Do you want it the same size, or bigger?" Finley asked.

"Bigger by a foot," Quinn requested.

"You got it. I'll need to go buy the wood, and I'll do the work out back so I don't get sawdust on anything." Finley walked over and started measuring the counter.

"I have an account at the hardware store. Just tell them to put the materials on my bill," Quinn told him.

"Okay, be back in a few." Finley left, and she walked over to Jade.

"You going to introduce me?" Quinn asked, nodding toward the other people.

"Sure. Quinn, this is Maddox Brown, Paley Thomas, and her brother Rick Thomas. We're the Outcasts; at least that's what they call us."

"Well, it's nice to meet you guys. Are you here to help Jade set up her stuff?" Quinn asked.

"Yes, and you too if you need it. We heard how you're helping Jade, and we just wanted to come in and give you a hand if you need it," Paley told her with a smile. They all looked like good people to her. She had the feeling that the four of them could use a good friend, and she planned on being that for them.

"I'm glad to have you guys here today. That counter and wall is where I want to showcase Jade's purses, and if she'll go get her jewelry then she can use the cabinet for that. Jade, you have carte blanche on how you want to decorate your wall. I've seen your taste and I love it," Quinn told her. She watched as Jade smiled; that was exactly what she was hoping for.

"I'll go over here and start on the clothes. See you guys in a few." Quinn walked over to the clothes racks. She had a lot of stock out already, but there was still a pile of boxes that needed to be unloaded.

The day progressed quickly, and the more she got done the more excited she got every time she looked around. When she finished with the clothing, she started putting jewelry in the cases. She was sorting out the jewelry for a particular artist, and there was jewelry scattered all over the counter. Instead of picking it up, she used her magic to drag the bracelet she needed across the counter and into her hand. She bent down and put it inside the case just as one of Arden's guards, who'd come in to relieve someone, charged over.

"You're a witch?" the guard demanded.

Quinn smiled and nodded. "Yes, I'm a witch. Why?" She looked around, surprised at how scared the guard looked. Finley had paused in putting together parts to the counter he'd made; like her, he seemed to feel the tension in the air as the guard backed away from her, then pulled out his cell phone and walked outside.

"What was that about?" Finley asked.

"I'm a witch; I did some magic and I guess it freaked him out? But they're wolves—they have to know about witches too," Quinn answered, puzzled.

"Cool, I didn't know there were witches! That's amazing that you're a witch," Finley said.

Maddox Brown walked up and set his laptop down on the counter. "Nobody told you about the Alpha's dad, did they?" Apparently, Maddox had seen her do the magic too, but it didn't seem to bother him.

Quinn lifted her shoulder in a half shrug. "Nobody has told me much, except 'you can't go here,' and, 'you can't leave.'"

"Magic is forbidden in the pack. Maybe you should talk to Jade about it. The Alpha has a past with a witch." They all turned their heads as they heard the truck skid to a stop in front of the store.

Arden and Bane strode inside and looked around until their eyes fell on her. Arden's eyes turned yellow, and as he approached, Maddox slowly bowed his head and backed away. Finley and Quinn both stood their ground.

"You're not a witch, are you?" Arden asked. She could hear the disbelief in his voice.

"Yes," Quinn answered, and Arden and Bane both backed up a step. "What's wrong with that? You're a wolf, and I'm a wolf now, but I'm also a witch. My whole family is witches and wizards. So what?"

"Leave us." Arden ordered. Everyone complied except Finley. "That means you too, wolf."

"What are you planning on doing with Quinn?" Finley asked, stepping closer to her. So quickly that Quinn didn't have time to move, Arden jumped on top of Finley and knocked him to the floor. He'd been standing so close that he hit her too, and they all landed in a heap.

Arden had his claws out and wrapped around Finley's throat. "I'm the Alpha, pup. If you have a problem with that, we can either settle this outside, or you're free to join another pack, but you won't be challenging my authority again."

"Finley, I'm fine. Please stop, Arden." Quinn's worry for Finley came through in her voice, and she could tell Arden didn't like that either. She didn't care, though, because right now he was judging her for being a witch. Nothing seemed to be going right since she moved to this town, and she'd had enough.

"You're the Alpha, but I won't stand by and watch you hurt her because she's a witch. She hasn't done anything wrong." Finley's voice was controlled, but his eyes flashed with fury.

"It doesn't matter, Finley. He's not only a controlling asshole, but a bigot, too. I knew I should have kept driving past this town and found another place to settle. I felt like something was calling me here, but now I know it was a mistake." Quinn shocked them both as she jumped up and headed out the back door.

She walked outside to find the guard who'd called Arden standing in front of the stairs. "I need to get up to my apartment."

Before he moved he gave her a dirty look and muttered, "Witch."

She didn't know why, but the fact that he was calling her that like it was an insult made her explode. "Son of a bitch!" Quinn yelled, then attacked the guard. Before she was aware of what she'd done, she had the guard on the ground with his hands behind his back.

Arden, Bane, and Finley ran outside and found Quinn on top of Jacks. "Don't you ever call me that again like it's something for me to be ashamed of. I'm not ashamed of being a witch any more then you should be ashamed that you're a wolf. You idiot."

Arden and Finley pulled her off, and then Arden grabbed Jacks' neck and lifted him off the ground. "You dare to touch my mate?"

"I swear. *Now* I'm his mate?" Quinn stormed up the steps and slammed the door behind her.

*****

Bane slowly approached Arden. "Alpha, let's find out what happened first, before you do something you might regret."

"What did you do to her, Jacks?" Arden demanded. His body was vibrating with rage, thinking that one of his guards had hurt Quinn. He lowered Jacks to the ground as he gasped for air.

"I never touched her, Alpha. I swear. I didn't know she was your mate. I wouldn't hurt a woman. I did call her a witch, but I swear that was all. Then she jumped me. Never seen a wolf move that fast except you and Bane," Jacks answered, rubbing his throat.

"She jumped you?" Bane asked with a chuckle.

"Hey she's strong, and fast. I hate to say it but your mate got the best of me. Had me on the ground before I knew what was going on. I shouldn't have said that to her, anyway. She didn't do anything except show me kindness since I got here today. She called in lunch for us and everything. But when I saw her do magic, it...it scared me. It made me think of your dad, and what happened to him. I'm sorry, Alpha."

Arden inhaled deeply, calming his wolf down. He'd reacted before he knew what was going on. That wasn't like him, and he knew it was the mating pull and not being able to touch her. "You can apologize later; first I need to calm down. Bane, make sure she doesn't leave until I can talk to her. I'll be back later."

Arden took off his clothes and left them on the stairs, then shifted and ran off into the woods. He knew where he needed to go to work this out. It didn't take him long to get to the old house where his father and mother had lived. The house was falling apart a bit, but it was still beautiful. His mom had put in a lot of work into the yard, planting flowers everywhere. He would sit beside her and help her put flowers into the pots that sat on the front porch.

The house was built for his mother; she'd wanted a house that looked like something from the Victorian age. The house was painted white, with huge columns in the front. A huge porch that wrapped all the way around the house, with lots of rocking chairs where the pack would gather when they had cook-outs. But nobody ever came here anymore, because of what had happened.

Arden shifted and went and sat down on the front steps. How could his mate be a witch? Was this some type of sick joke? He remembered what his dad had said to him when he found out the young girl had killed herself; he said that it didn't matter what you were, everyone had problems. But she'd wanted to be a wolf desperately, and that disturbed his dad. Apparently she hated being a witch. Arden remembered her watching them all the time, enthralled by how the wolves acted around each other. She'd liked that they were always hugging each other, and she wanted a family like that. But his father couldn't have turned her even if he wanted to. The Council only allowed human mates to be turned.

"My mate is a witch, Dad, how do you like that?" Arden chuckled, a little bitterly, as he looked up at the house. He sighed. "She's already everything to me, but she scares the hell out of me. How can that be? Magic? My mate can do magic, Dad. I wish you were here. I could use a huge dose of wisdom right now."

Arden could feel the cold breeze blow across his face as he closed his eyes. It almost felt like his mother's hand when she would calm his nerves. Anytime he got angry or in trouble for something, his mom would touch his face as he closed his eyes. "I hope that's you, Mom. I think you'd like her. She reminds me of you, and how strong you were. She doesn't take anything from anyone, including me."

Arden sat like that for a couple of hours, thinking about what to do about Quinn. Lord, the woman had a temper, but so did he. And she was a witch. How could he live with a witch, knowing what one had done to his dad? He needed guidance, and even though his parents weren't here, he could still feel them as if they were.

He still loved this old place; he wished they could fix it up and use it for something. The roses were still growing all around it. Arden knew what he needed to do. Giving in wasn't in his nature, but like his mom always said, 'Sometimes you have to give a little, baby boy, and let others help you lead.' Quinn would be a great leader, he thought. Right now she needed to spread her wings and get her store off the ground, and that's where he needed to be to help her. So now it was time for him to face the music—and man, did he hate that. He wanted to stay and hide a little longer, but he'd been gone for a while and needed to get back.

Arden rushed back to town. It was already getting dark outside. Most of the wolves were hidden, patrolling the property, except for his Beta. Bane was sitting on the steps like he didn't have a care in the world.

"Well, did you get it worked out?" Bane asked as he puffed on a cigar.

"Somewhat. I ran for a while, and that helped." Arden put his clothes back on and sat down beside him. "Has she come back out?"

"Nope, but I could hear her banging around up there and cussing you like the mangy dog you are," Bane said with a grin.

"Mangy dog, eh? Wow, she knows she's a wolf now too, right?" Arden said jokingly.

"Yeah, but I think it was you specifically she was cursing."

They both sat silently for a while until Arden asked, "What would you do, Bane, if you found out your mate was a witch? Like the one person who destroyed your family?"

"If the fates had given me a witch, bear, or a mangy dog, I guess I would accept it, because they do that for a reason. Maybe she can help you. I don't know, to be honest, but I know she's your mate and you need to respect that." Bane didn't mince his words. He was blunt and to the point—often with a joke mixed in, but he always made sense.

"Guess I need to go and talk to her." Arden sighed, but didn't move from the stairs. "Did you send Jacks home?"

"Yeah. I thought since he got put on his ass by the Alpha's mate he needed a break, but he wanted to apologize to Quinn. I told him maybe tomorrow, and to go home and get some rest in the meantime." Bane explained as he blew smoke rings in the air.

"Good." Arden got up and started up the stairs, then turned around. "You should've seen her, Bane. Man, she had him on the ground with his hands behind his back before he knew what hit him."

Bane and Arden both started laughing.

"Guess it's my time to get put on my ass." Arden walked up the stairs and knocked on the door.

He was either going to drive her away, or she would understand why he'd been so upset to find out she was a witch.

Chapter 7

Arden knocked on the door, but as he did the door swung open. He needed to fix that. "Bane, get me a tool box so I can fix the lock on this door," he called down. Opening the door up, Arden looked around the room and found Quinn sitting in a rocking chair, watching him.

"Your door came open. I'll fix it for you." Arden said, then walked in and sat down across from her. "We need to talk, Quinn. I think you need to know why you being a witch freaks everyone out." He waited for a response, but didn't get one.

He sighed, and started explaining, "When I was very young and my father was the Alpha of the Dixon pack, he was approached by the daughter of a local witch. She was just seventeen years old, but apparently she hated being a witch because they never loved on her or appreciated her in any way. She would sit and watch all of us, and you could tell that she was desperate for any attention. She didn't make it a secret that she wanted to be turned, but it's against our laws to turn a human unless he or she is mate to a wolf. Then the Alpha informs the Council, and they bring a representative down to witness the turning. As you've found out, it can be very painful and some have even died. The representative will make sure that the human is one hundred percent on board with this.

"When Tabitha Ross turned eighteen years old she approached my father and asked him to turn her. She said that her mother didn't love her, and she wanted to be in a pack like the wolves were. My father felt sorry for the girl, but he couldn't grant her wish. He tried talking to her, but she just started to cry and left. Nobody heard from her or saw her again until a week later, when her body was found hanging outside our house. She'd got on pack land somehow, using magic to mask her scent, then she tied a rope around her neck and jumped from the tree.

"She left a note saying that it was my father's fault. That was all her mother needed, the name of someone to blame. Instead of realizing that her daughter had problems and she'd contributed to those problems, she focused on getting revenge. So in her sick mind she conjured up a spell, and sent it to my father—to make him kill his only son while in wolf form. She hated my father and wanted to punish him, and in her view it made sense to take away his only son.

"The day the spell took effect, his Beta—Bane's father, Tex—was walking by the house and heard my mother screaming. My father had shifted and tried to attack me, but my mother could see something was wrong with his wolf and intervened. She protected me, but my father killed her while trying to get in the door. Tex called out to the other guards, and they subdued him until they could figure out what went wrong. The witch had to be on our land to cast the spell, so the guards tracked her down and locked her up. When they called the Council to tell them what had happened, the Council sent the Death Hunters. Since my father had killed my mother, he was put to death right along with the witch."

"Why would the Death Hunters do that, knowing that your father was under a spell? It wasn't his fault, he wasn't in his right mind." Quinn finally spoke, sounding shocked.

"It didn't matter to them, because he'd killed my mother. My father was distraught. When they killed the witch it broke the spell, and my father was inconsolable. I lost both of my parents because of a witch, and the pack lost their leaders. They loved my mom and dad, and I had to grow up early. Tex ran the pack until I was old enough to take over. But I made a vow that no witches were allowed in our community, and we've never had one since, until you showed up."

"You have to know that there are good witches and bad ones, just like with wolves and every other being on earth. You're judging me for something I didn't do and never would. How is that fair? I didn't choose to be a wolf, and you just accepted me and Finley like it was nothing, but the fact that I'm a witch as well makes it different?" Quinn stopped rocking and stared at him.

"Did you not hear the story?" Arden asked.

"Yes, Arden. Did *you* not hear what I just said?" Quinn got up and stood in front of the chair. "What do you expect me to do? Pack up and leave because you're scared?"

Arden jumped up. "I'm not scared, Quinn, but you need to understand how we all feel."

"So I'll ask again, what do you want me to do?" Arden could see her hands shaking as she waited for his answer.

"Quinn, you're my mate, but you need to realize that the pack isn't going to be so understanding. Some may try to challenge you, and you're not ready for that. You're strong, but not strong enough, and I don't want to see you get hurt. Just lay off the magic around the pack, until—"

"Until what, Arden? Until they start to like me?"

"That's not fair, Quinn. I'm trying here, and I don't see you doing the same. Give me a little break."

Quinn knew she was being a bitch, but he started all of this. She meant no harm to anyone, and would never send out a spell like that. There was a code in the Craft, rules to follow, and one of them was to never do spells against an innocent person.

"For now, Arden. We have rules too, but just like you and your kind we have those who don't follow the rules and cause evil wherever they go. But I'm a witch just as much as a wolf, and sometimes my magic wants out just like my wolf. I do understand their fear, but you have to tell them that if they try me, they might find out I'm stronger then they thought."

"Fair enough." He wanted to kiss her, but she was still mad, and he didn't want to get his face scratched off. "I'm going to fix your door, and you have a store downstairs that needs putting together." Arden smiled, then went over to the door and opened it. Bane was standing right outside, with cigar in one hand and a toolbox in the other. "Did you hear all that?"

"Heard enough, Alpha. I think I'll go for a run and then come back for the night shift." Bane smiled unrepentantly and walked down the steps. Arden shook his head at his Beta. He was a character, to say the least, and Arden couldn't wait for him to find his mate, because when he did Arden was going to rub it in every chance he got.

"Thanks for fixing the door." Quinn tried to squeeze by him, but her touch was all it took for him to drop the toolbox, push her against the wall, and kiss her. Being this close to her was hard. He needed to touch and taste her before she left to go downstairs.

Quinn tried to pull away, but her body disobeyed her. Her lips were so soft as they swept across his. The kiss ended too quickly, and he pulled away.

"Thanks for listening," Arden said, then allowed her to walk away.

******

Arden felt as if he'd won the lottery. He drove back to the pack house with a huge smile on his face. He could still feel their kiss as he touched his lips again. She tasted like he'd thought she would: sweet, like vanilla and chocolate. Her fiery red hair and her temper made who she was, and she was special. He parked and walked inside the pack house, planning to take a shower then do a little work in his office.

As he entered his bedroom, his thoughts were on his mate, and he didn't notice Alice at first. When he looked up, she was standing beside his bed, naked. *Damn, this isn't what I wanted tonight.* "Alice, what are you doing?"

"Waiting for you." Alice purred as she stalked toward him. Before he could say anything, she'd already wrapped around him and started rubbing herself all over him.

"Alice, stop."

"Come on, lover, I know you want it as much as I do." Alice continued to rub all over him until he threw her on the bed.

"Get out, Alice. I've found my mate, and you know that. You know how this works. When we find our mate that's all we can think about, and Quinn's my mate. I don't want to have this conversation with you again. Get your clothes on and get out." Arden was finished being nice with her. Alice was a troublemaker, and he could kick himself in the teeth for even having sex with her in the first place.

"She's a witch, from what I hear. Has she put a spell on you?" Alice was touching his face, and it was pissing him off now.

"Yes she is, but she's a wolf too, and most importantly she's my mate and soon to be your Alpha," Arden growled. "Stop touching me and get out, Alice. She's not like the last one. Maybe if you got to know her you might like her."

Alice sat on the bed with her arms crossed. "I doubt it," she muttered.

"You better get used to it," Arden finished, and walked into his bathroom and locked the door. He waited until he heard his bedroom door open and close again before he turned the shower on. He needed to talk with Bane about Alice. If he knew her as well as he thought he did, she'd try to start trouble with Quinn, and Quinn wasn't ready for a wolf like Alice. The woman had been fighting every girl who came of age for years, letting them know she was in charge. Unfortunately, that was the way it worked in the pack: everyone fought for position, and Alice made sure she won.

Eventually, Quinn would have to fight Alice, to show her that she was the Alpha. He only hoped that Quinn would be strong enough to beat her. If not, Alice would challenge her, and he didn't know what he would do about that. Right now he had too many other things to worry about.

Quinn walked back in the store and saw that Jade, Rick, Paley, and Maddox were sitting around a small table, reading books. She smiled, because they were all quiet, concentrating intensely. She realized that Jade was right about putting a coffee space to the side of the store. It wouldn't take away from the store; in fact, it would bring in more business if men had a place they could sit and drink coffee and read while their wives shopped. She could order some coffee machines and put in some bookshelves. Maybe start small and then add to it later.

"Hey, Jade." Jade and her group looked up at Quinn. "Maybe you were right about putting in a coffee shop right here in the store, with some books and tables in it. Give the men a place to sit while their women shop."

"Really? Oh, Quinn, we have it all planned out! In fact, we've researched a place to get the coffeemakers and an espresso machine to make different types of coffee. This is great... Oh, I almost forgot the books! Everyone around here reads, Quinn, and if you got some good books in, it would bring a lot more customers." Jade's hands were clasped together, and she had a huge smile on her face.

"You seem to have it all under control, so that can be your job then. Find me the stuff and let me see how much it's going to cost. Then we can order it. Maybe we can get at least some of it here by tomorrow." Quinn could see that Jade and her friends were happy, and that made her happy too. Rick pulled out his laptop, and they completely ignored her while they started getting quotes up and researching.

She decided she had a lot of other things to do and left them to complete that project. Finley was putting up some shelves, and she had some more boxes to unpack. There was so much more to do, and they were short on time.

She heard the bell go off at the front of store and watched a blonde-haired woman walk in, a group of girls with her. The way they acted when they spotted Jade at her jewelry counter made Quinn tense. She knew these were the girls who'd made Jade's life hell, and she wasn't going to put up with it. Especially here in her store.

She walked slowly over to Jade, listening to find out what they were doing there. "Well look at old Scarface and her ugly purses and jewelry. Really Jade, do you honestly believe anyone will buy this crap?" Alice and her group of friends giggled.

Quinn walked over with a huge smile on her face. "Jade, I just got some great news for you. The lady who sells a lot of my stuff in New York said she wanted more of your purses, and she wants to see the jewelry line. I sent her some pictures and she loves what she is seeing, so we have to get more to send her. You're going to be a success, my friend. I'm so happy for you!" Quinn hugged Jade, then glanced over at Alice. She could see the other girls frown, then look at the purses hanging on the walls and back at Jade.

"Oh sorry, hello. I couldn't wait to tell Jade the great news. She's going to be selling her products like crazy." Quinn smiled big for the whopper of a lie she just told. "I don't think we've met. I'm Quinn, and welcome to Southern Treasures. You must be part of the pack."

"You're the witch." Alice's voice was snarky, and she smirked after saying it.

Quinn giggled. "Well I'm a wolf now, too, but yes, I'm a witch." Apparently, nobody ever stood up to Alice, because she looked completely taken aback that Quinn wasn't backing down.

"You may have the Alpha fooled, but we all know what you'll do. You're not his mate, because if you were he wouldn't be fucking me."

The frown left her face, and Quinn didn't like where this was going. She'd believed Arden when he said she was his mate, but now one of his exes was saying she was still sleeping with him?

"He is? Oh well, I hope you're having a great time then." Quinn acted like it didn't bother her, and waited to see what Alice would say now. Except it did bother her, and right now she wanted to punch this bitch in the face.

Alice walked over toward her and got real close. "Seeing that you're half wolf now, I bet you can smell Arden on me. We just had sex before I came here. Come on, take a big whiff."

Quinn wanted to knock her into next week, but she was trying to stay in control here, even though her wolf was clawing to get out. She inhaled deeply to try and calm down, but what she smelled almost knocked her down. Alice was right; she could smell Arden on her.

"Alice, the Alpha is going to be mad," Jade was trying to help, but it was true. Arden's scent was all over Alice.

"Can it, Scarface. Miss Witch here needs to realize that she has competition. I will challenge you everywhere you go." Alice was jerked back when Bane grabbed hold of her from behind.

"Alice, I don't know what kind of games you're playing, but the Alpha has declared no challenges until we find and handle the rogues. Get out of the store. You have no business here." Bane growled the last part, and Alice and her friends all walked out.

When the doors closed, Bane shook his head. "I hope you know how to fight because that one is going to need to be taken down or she'll continue to be this way forever."

"Why do I have to know how to fight? I haven't done anything to her," Quinn protested.

"Listen, Quinn, things are different for wolves. When we want a spot in the hierarchy, we fight for it. Like me being Beta. Just because my father was Beta didn't mean that I would inherit the position. The moment Arden announced that I was his choice to be Beta, I got challenged. I won, of course, but after about the tenth time, I told them the next one would be to the death and nobody challenged me again. Arden was different, because all of his were to the death.

"Alice has fought her way up, and she's the head bitch in charge in the pack, literally. No other female out-ranks her, and she does like being in power. Maybe too much. I've been watching her, and she definitely needs to be challenged and taken down. All Alice wants to do is belittle the females and tell them what to do. She's not a real leader."

"I know how to do some fighting, but not in wolf form. I don't get it," Quinn said with a sigh.

"I know there are a lot of things you'll have to get used to, Quinn, but Alice isn't a wolf you'd want to meet in a dark alley. From what I saw when you were first turned, you're a natural-born fighter, and if you're interested I can help you out with this." Bane shrugged. "But it's up to you."

Judging by the way Bane spoke about Alice, and from what she'd seen already, the woman was going to be a problem. The issue at hand, though, was why she smelled of Arden. She must have misread him when he kissed her, and all this crap about being mates wasn't true. She needed to ask about this mate thing from someone other than Arden. Apparently he couldn't stop screwing the women in his pack.

"I have some time once I unload this box. You got a minute for some questions?" Quinn asked.

"Sure."

"Good, but let's go over here so we can talk in private." Quinn walked over to where her office was going to be, and allowed Bane to go in first. She closed the door, then sat down behind her desk. "I have some questions about mates, and the pack in general."

"What kind of questions?" Bane waited. She could tell he was eager to talk about pack life with her, which was good because she wanted some personal answers, too.

"I haven't gotten a chance to meet anyone much, but how many are in the pack?" Quinn asked.

"Before you and Finley we had one hundred and nineteen. That includes the Elders and the young pups."

"Elders?"

"We have older wolves who act as Elders for the pack. They know and keep all the history of the pack. Some of the younger pack members are away at college—we're not just country bumpkins—but most come back here and bring back the knowledge they got from college, or they meet their mate and join another pack. We have a festival here during Christmas, and so far two packs are joining us. We have all kinds of events and just some fun times. It gives the wolves a chance to meet others and maybe meet their mates. So far ten pack members have met their mates that way. Some stay here, and some go to the other packs."

"You said something about Alice being head bitch. What does that mean?" Quinn asked.

"Well, we have a hierarchy here in the pack. You have the Alpha, of course, and then the Beta, which is me. Then we have Lieutenants or Guards. There's a similar hierarchy for the females, and since we didn't have an Alpha's mate—which is you, by the way—Alice challenged everyone who was even a contender. She keeps things running pretty smoothly, and no one's complained about her."

"Hell, Bane, they're scared to. Do you know what she calls your sister?" Quinn asked, and the smile fell off Bane's face. "She calls her Scarface. That bitch has made your sister's life miserable, and all the other kids her age, too. She's threatened by them. So what if they're different; hell, I'm different. I don't like her, and when I get the chance she won't have to worry about challenging me because I'm going to knock her down all on my own."

Quinn stopped and took a deep breath. "Let's talk about something else. So, I take it that since you haven't found your mate yet, you go out like normal people and date and have sex a lot?"

Bane laughed. "Of course we have sex. Look, here it is in the simplest of terms: we can date, or have sex with, as many women as we want, but once we find our mate things are different. Our mate is our lifeline, our soul mate. Once we find our mate, we'll never want another female like we will our mate. All we think about is our mate: we think about sex with our mates, but we also dwell on their safety, who they're with, or even who is touching them. That's why Arden gets crazy around you."

"You're wrong about me and Arden being mates. You see, you just answered a lot of questions for me." Quinn knew something was going on, and Arden was wrong, or lying, about them being mates.

"No you're wrong, you're the Alpha's mate." Bane narrowed his eyes at her in confusion.

"No, because if Arden was my mate then he wouldn't still be sleeping with Alice. I know what Arden smells like, and she was drenched in him. She even told me that she just left his bed. He must do the old 'mate' thing with all the new wolves so he can get them in bed. Make no mistake; this is one wolf that he won't have. Now let's go practice."

Bane got up without saying anything. He looked just as confused as he walked out of the office. "We can go over to the gym. I know nobody is using the room in the basement, and I have the keys to lock up the doors so nobody will see us."

"Okay, let me tell Finley and Jade that I'll be back in a few." Quinn walked off. Even though Bane had explained how it worked, she was sick over knowing that Arden had lied to her. And apparently Bane, too, since he'd looked just as shocked at what she said.

Chapter 8

Bane walked into Arden's office, frowning. "Are you still fucking Alice?"

Arden looked up. "What are you talking about? You know that Quinn is my mate. I'm just giving her some time to get used to being turned before I jump her bones. So, hell no, and why are you even asking?"

"Because Quinn told me earlier that you were still screwing the women in the pack and that you must tell all the women that they're your mate so you can have sex with them."

"What?" Arden yelled.

"Just saying that you need to get that under control, because if you don't you might not have a mate soon," Bane warned him.

"What the hell happened? After I left she was smiling, and I thought she enjoyed the kiss and…other things." Arden put his head in his hands and let out a deep sigh. "I think I'm losing my touch."

Bane chuckled. "No, I think you have a certain wolf who doesn't want to let you go because she knows she won't be the HBIC anymore."

Arden picked his head up and frowned. "You're so strange. What does HBIC mean?"

"You know, 'Head Bitch in Charge.'" When Arden continued to stare at him, Bane rolled his eyes. "You know, *Alice*."

"There are times when I have to ask myself why you're my second in command." Arden asked, still confused.

"Come on, dude. Alice came into the store today and she smelled like you and she rubbed it in Quinn's face. Quinn is a new wolf; I'm sure the mating pull is something strange to her and she doesn't realize what she's feeling because she is feeling so much right now. Hell, her body is going haywire with scents, but I bet she smelled you on her."

"Shit, I should've known she was up to something. Earlier today, I found Alice in my bedroom, naked, and before I knew what she was doing, she rubbed all over me. Shit, I bet she did it on purpose." Arden got up.

"Where are you going?"

"To see my mate and explain this." Arden answered, walking out the door. "Also, don't forget about the patrols tonight. I want this pack found and dealt with."

"Yeah, yeah old wise one," Bane muttered.

Arden decided that it was time for his mate to understand that she was it for him. He shifted and ran to the store, hoping to explain everything. What he wasn't expecting was to see his guard Pete Moss looking in the store window like a stalker. He turned around and frowned when Arden shifted and stepped up on the porch.

"What are you doing?" Arden asked.

"She's crying," Pete said, concerned. "I heard her and came to check on her. She was on the phone, and then she started crying."

Arden looked in the window and watched as Quinn laid her head down on the table, boxes scattered around her. He could hear her pain as she sobbed. He knocked on the window, and Quinn looked around until she saw him. He pointed toward the door. For a minute he thought she wasn't going to open it, but she got herself together and unlocked it.

"What's wrong?" he asked.

"Nothing. I'm just tired," Quinn answered, but he could tell she'd been crying for a while.

Arden pushed himself inside and then closed the door behind him. "I'm not screwing around with Alice."

"What?"

"I'm not screwing Alice. Not since I first saw you," Arden repeated.

"Well, she sure smelled like you, but it's none of my business who you have sex with." Quinn waved him off then walked back to the table and started unpacking some candles. He could see her jaw tense up and her mouth was pursed angrily. She was trying to keep it together, but he could see it did matter to her.

"Of course it's your business. I'm your mate." Arden didn't understand why that was so hard for her, but he could hear his mother telling him that just because he thought something, it didn't always mean that others felt the same way. He needed to show her how he felt.

"Look, she already told me she'd just come from your bed, and she smelled of you, so you don't have to make up lies."

"Lies! I'm not lying." Arden pulled her hands to him. "Listen." He lowered his voice. "Earlier, after I left here and went home, I found Alice in my bedroom naked, and she jumped on me. I should've known she was up to something when she kept rubbing all over me even after I told her to leave. I threw her off me and told her that you were my mate."

"You did?" Quinn asked, surprised.

"Of course. I couldn't have sex with her. Hell woman, I can never have sex with anyone but you. Nobody will ever make me feel like you do," Arden explained as he walked over to her and gently wiped away her tears. "Nobody will ever be as beautiful as you. I only see you, and I only want you." Tears fell down her face as she listened. "Why are you so sad?"

Quinn swallowed hard and closed her eyes. "Because my father hates me."

He shook his head. "Nobody could hate you, Quinn." Arden pushed her hair away from her face and tucked it behind her ears.

"My father does. He'd rather see me married to a man I don't want than see me happy, and I'm not going to marry someone I don't love," Quinn said.

"You're my mate, and I won't let you marry another man," Arden answered, but he could feel his wolf pushing to get to her. The mere mention of another man with his mate made him defensive and almost crazed. But he had to remember that Quinn was a young wolf and wouldn't understand how he was feeling. It would scare her, and he couldn't let that happen. *Calm yourself, old boy,* Arden said to his wolf.

"*You* won't. Don't you see that you're acting just like him when you say things like that to me? You don't own me, Arden. Why do you do that?" Quinn blew out her breath.

She was getting upset, so he needed to diffuse this. "Quinn, I'm not trying to take control. It's just who I am, and most wolves are like this. You will be too once you get older. You're still a young wolf. Look, I don't want to argue, but you need to get some of that frustration out before you explode on someone. Let's go run. The stars are out, and it's a great night. Come on." Arden pulled on her hand, leading her to the door. "Come on, you know you want to."

The corners of Quinn's eyes crinkled as a small smile spread across her face. "Take off your clothes, and we can leave from here. I want to show you a place."

Arden opened the door. "Pete, we're going running. Lock up the store and we'll be back later." When he turned back around, Quinn had already shifted and was waiting on him.

"You're getting fast, little wolf." Arden touched the end of her nose, then took off his clothes as she watched him get undressed. He smiled, then shifted and took off out the door. He didn't have to turn around to know she was following him.

Chapter 9

Quinn loved the feel of the wind brushing against her fur. This was exactly what she needed. What surprised her every time she shifted was how well she could communicate with her wolf. The wolf was inside her, and it felt like she was a separate person and yet like they were one at the same time.

Arden said that Alice was lying and that he hadn't had sex with her, but then why would she say that they had? She was such a bitch. But what goes around comes around, and she was going to be there when Alice got what was coming to her.

She knew they were on Dixon land because of the "No Trespassing" signs everywhere. They'd been running for a long time when Arden started slowing down. She was hot and sweaty, and she hoped wherever they were going she could get some water. That was a long run, and she was thirsty.

As they slowed down she could hear water flowing, and she could even smell the moisture in the air. Some kind of water was close by.

Arden came to a stop by a beautiful waterfall and pond. This place was wonderful and exotic, and all the wildflowers growing around it made it more alluring to explore, but right now all she wanted was some water. She followed Arden as he waded out in the pond and drank. She mirrored his actions, and then water splashed all over her, soaking her fur.

Shaking the water off, Quinn watched as Arden emerged from the water. Wow. She blinked several times, because the man was magnificent. Not only was he tall, he was the finest specimen she'd ever met, and his body was to die for. His black hair glowed in the moonlight. He hadn't shaved and she loved that about him. She wanted to reach out and touch the stubble on his face. She ached as he emerged further from the water, and a 'v' of hair appeared, going down below the water. Any time he was around, her hormones went crazy.

"Shift and get in. I'll even turn around if you need me to." Arden smiled, and then actually turned around.

Quinn thought about it for a second, then figured 'what the hell.' She shifted and went underwater. Lord have mercy, the water felt wonderful. It was cool to her heated skin as she poked her head above the water. She looked up to find Arden watching her like she was going to disappear. Then she realized he could actually see her ample breasts as they remained just above the surface.

Damn, she never realized just how much they floated. She put her arms over her chest and eased back a little. It was dark outside, but she knew they both could see in the dark.

"So, you ever been dunked underwater?" Arden asked, playfully easing closer to her.

"You stop right there," Quinn commanded, but Arden continued to swim a little closer until he was right up against her, and whispered, "I'm sorry Quinn, but I have to kiss you."

Arden pressed his lips briefly against hers. She could tell he was gauging whether or not she was going to allow him to continue, and the answer was yes she was. She licked the top of his lips, letting him know he had his answer. Pulling her closer to him in the water, he massaged a spot on her shoulder where he would eventually bite her and make her his. But he already knew she wasn't ready for that, not yet. He needed to stop when he felt his canines lengthen. Once her legs wrapped around his waist, Arden took control as he carried her over to the waterfall then went under it.

Quinn opened her eyes and found they'd entered a small cave with beautiful rocks inside. As he carried her she could feel his erection rubbing against her, making her body ache more for him. It had been so long, and everywhere he touched ignited her body. Lifting her higher, Arden placed her on top of the cool rocks. Her legs fell open, and he jumped up and pushed between them. His tongue ran from one breast to another as his lips captured her nipple.

"Please, don't stop." Quinn shuddered as his hand kneaded her other breast. She couldn't control her body as she wiggled underneath him. She was ready.

"I need you now, Arden." Quinn arched her back as his lips left her breast. He pulled her legs closer to him and slid one finger inside, and that was all it took to make Quinn scream out her orgasm, the sound echoing around them in the small space. His eyes glowed as he watched her reaction.

"I love watching you," Arden said before he slowly pushed himself inside and waited. Quinn gasped as she suddenly realized that Arden was huge. "Sorry, I'm having a hard time keeping myself under control. I want you so bad, Quinn. I want to fuck you so hard, but I'm afraid I'm going to hurt you."

Slowly, he pulled out, then pushed back in, setting an agonizingly slow pace. "Arden, please...."

"You ready for me, baby?" Arden tortured her with his voice.

"Yes, *now*."

"Your wish is granted." Arden pushed as far inside as he could. As he continued to thrust, he seemed to go further each time, hitting that spot that made her crazy. So crazy, Quinn's claws came out, digging into his back. If she kept that up he would surely mark her.

Arden grabbed her hands and held them over her head, then pounded into her. "Baby you feel so good and tight." He leaned down and sucked a nipple inside his mouth, and she lost it all over again. Her whole body came apart as he continued to hit her g-spot over and over again until she came again. These sensation took her breath away as he reached his climax and exploded inside of her.

They lay silently together until they could get up. The water was cool as it splashed across the smooth rocks, and the anxiety and tension she'd been feeling earlier was now gone. He was right again. Damn, he would use that against her.

"You okay?" Arden's voice sounded as satisfied as she felt.

"Better. Thank you."

Arden chuckled. "We need to do this more often."

Laughing, she said, "I guess we should. Beats going to the gym and working out."

"Honey, as a wolf you'll never have to go to a gym again as long as you let her run when she wants to." He reached over and ran his fingers down between her breasts. "But it's not like you need to worry about working on your body. It's perfect."

"You really mean that?" Quinn asked.

"Are you...you don't see how beautiful you are, do you?" Arden asked.

"I don't think I'm ugly, but I never really focused on my appearance. I'm not a conceited person. I mean, don't get me wrong, I want to look pretty, but I just don't stress over it." Quinn leaned up and looked around. "It's beautiful under here."

"It is."

"I need to get back, Arden. I have a lot to get done," Quinn said reluctantly. She leaned over and kissed him on the lips, then jumped in the water.

*****

Arden walked into the conference room and shut the door. Bane and all of his command staff were waiting for him. He could still smell Quinn on himself, and he loved it. She smelled like cotton candy. She also had some candles in the shop that smelled just like her. He'd asked if he could buy one from her, and she smiled and gave it to him. He wanted it in his bedroom so he would smell her all the time.

"Looks like someone is happy." Bane joked, then leaned over and inhaled. "Ah, now I see why."

"Shut up," Arden joked back, but he wanted all of his men to know that Quinn was his mate. He wanted them to be familiar with her scent, especially on him. "Let's get this meeting started. We have a lot to discuss. First, yes, I have found my mate, and most of you already met her. Her name is Quinn Lamone, and here's the big news—she's a witch, too." He figured he would hear groans and moans about that, but nobody said anything. "I figured at least one of you would say something about Quinn being my mate and also a witch."

Pete Moss looked around the room at the others before he spoke. "Alpha, I met your mate, and I like her a lot. I think she'll make a great fit, but since nobody is going to say anything, I will. It's some of the pack that will be scared of her. You might need to talk with them and tell them before the rumor mill gets started. I already heard Alice and her bunch making up lies about Quinn to some of the older wolves. I think you might want to have a meeting with the pack and tell everyone about it all together."

"Thanks for being honest, Pete. I was planning on doing that in a few. Quinn is having a grand opening today, and I want security tight in the city but also here on pack grounds. I don't want these rogues to feel like we're not on our game. I'll need to go over some rules for tomorrow, too."

"What worries me the most is the fact that we haven't seen or heard anything from this pack since Quinn was bitten. Bane has a schedule worked out, and you'll all be assigned posts. We need to be on the look-out for anything strange. I don't want any humans being taken tomorrow. The chief of police is going to be out with his guys, too. Let's make sure we're all on our game, because a lot of people will be there." Arden stood up and smiled at his men. "Thank you all for all of your hard work. I have a feeling that it's going to be a good week; let's make it great for the pack."

Arden's command staff all stood up and agreed. They each hugged Arden and congratulated him on finding his mate, then left the room.

He sat back down with Bane. "Do you think the pack is going to give Quinn a hard time?"

"I don't know; only time will tell. We need to shut Alice up before she whips the whole pack into a frenzy, though," Bane added. "I hope she isn't going to turn out like that woman in *Fatal Attraction*. You know, where she kills the kid's pet bunny, puts it in a pot on the stove, and when they come home the mom finds it in there and screams. You're not a screamer, are you?"

Arden stared at Bane. The man could come up with some crazy shit. "I don't have a pet bunny, Bane, so I think I'm okay."

"Yeah, but what if she just puts one in there for like, shock value? What if Quinn comes home from a hard day at work and finds a dead bunny boiling on the stove? Do you think Alice is that crazy?"

"I don't even know what to say to you right now," Arden said, shaking his head as he stood up.

"You say that now, my friend, but when you find the dead bunny rabbit on the stove, you'll remember this conversation!" Bane yelled out as Arden left the room.

Later that morning, Arden waited in the open field for the pack to gather. He watched as Alice and her group showed up smirking. He had to deal with her after the meeting or she was going to be a big problem.

"Good morning, pack." It was still early and Arden needed to hurry this along, so that everything was in place before Quinn opened her doors at noon. "I know you have heard a lot of rumors lately, and I want to tell you the truth since some have been viciously spreading lies." He looked over at Alice, who had the common sense to look down at the ground. "This week I met my mate." Arden waited as some of the pack members who hadn't heard anything started clapping. "Thank you. Her name is Quinn Lamone, and she recently moved to town and purchased Charlotte's Closet. She's re-opening it today, as Southern Treasures."

"Alpha, isn't your mate a witch?" Alice yelled out so everyone could hear her. The crowd, who were excited five seconds ago, now were gasping and covering their mouths. She looked around, nodding when other pack members glanced over at her for confirmation.

"Yes, Alice, and if you could let me finish I'll explain to the pack what is going on." The look he gave her wasn't close to what he was going to do as soon as this meeting was over. "Quinn is a witch, and comes from a long line of witches who are part of the Witches and Wizards Council. Her father is an elder in the WWC. She is not the kind of witch who would do me or any of you harm. I've told her about Beatrice Hoffman, and what she did to my dad. I know it will take some time for all of you to get used to a witch being around us again, but as you know we have no choice in our fated mate.

"She has the grand opening today for her store at noon. I would appreciate it if you could stop by and at least introduce yourself. Remember, we support our own, and Quinn and Finley Egan were both bitten by the rogue pack this week and turned. So we still need to be on the look-out for that pack. There will be a lot of humans in town this weekend, so keep your eyes open."

"How do we know she isn't that kind of witch?" Alice asked, trying to provoke the pack. He looked over at Bane, and he could tell his friend's wolf was pushing out. He wanted to make her submit too.

"Alice, since you're continuing with this agenda to make my mate look bad, I think it's only fair to tell the pack about the lies you've been spreading. First, you show up in my bedroom naked and jump me so you can get your scent on me. Then, when I ordered you to leave, you went to my mate's workplace and told her we're still sleeping together and you just left my bed."

"Then, when that didn't work, you and a select few—who will be dealt with later—showed up here and went around to as many pack members you could to try and turn them against Quinn. She has done nothing to you, Alice. She's just trying to run a business and bring more people to our community to buy our goods. You should be ashamed of yourself." Arden watched as members of the pack glared at her; some wouldn't even look at her. His point was made, harsh as it was. She'd given him no choice, though. "Alice, you and your group will wait by the pack house and I'll deal with you in a bit. You are all dismissed."

Arden waited until they were gone before starting the meeting up again. "Pack, a lot of changes are going on. We still have dangers among us, but what we have to do is stick together and not allow animosity to interfere with our pack and what is best for us. Fear can make a person do stupid things. I've gotten to know Quinn and she's not like Beatrice. I want you to meet her and make your own judgment instead of letting lies do that for you. To grow, we need mates, and to stay strong we have to believe in one another. If you have any concerns, please come to me and we can sit down and work them out like we always have. Again, if you would try and support Quinn during this time, I would appreciate it. I think once you've met her you'll find that she's like us and only wants this to work out."

"The store is opening today at noon. Also, Jade Cross will have her purse and jewelry line at Southern Treasures. She has already sold a good bit through Quinn's online shop. Stop by and support Jade and Quinn, and the other pack members who are working there. Ms. Nelly, I know you have quilts that you make for the fairs, and I bet if you talk to Quinn she could find a spot in the store which can bring in more business for you." Arden waited and saw that some of the Elders smiled and patted Ms. Nelly on the back as they all left. Her mate had passed away, and she needed something to keep her going. Making quilts was something she liked to do, and it helped bring in money for her to live on.

"What do you think?" Arden asked Bane.

"I think it went great, but you still need to do something about Alice and the others for trying to start trouble. Plus, she was being rude while you were trying to conduct an official meeting. So I think cleaning up the common areas and bathrooms would be a good punishment for her and the group. I can go and check to make sure they're being done properly."

"Sounds good to me. Let's go give Alice the bad news." Arden smiled, thinking about Alice and the others cleaning all the bathrooms in the pack house and cleaning up after all the little ones in the common areas. It was always a disaster after the kids had been playing and using the bathrooms.

Chapter 10

Quinn looked around the store one last time, making sure everything was in place and that everyone she offered a job to was ready to go. She had Rick and Paley running the cash registers. Jade was manning her side of the store, with all the jewelry and purses. Finley had some friends who needed jobs, and she'd given them a crash course in sales. Most had worked odd jobs before, and picked it up pretty quickly. Especially Emily, who'd worked at a coffee shop in Atlanta. She wanted to run the coffee and book part of the store. Everything seemed to be in place and working out.

Why her thoughts seemed to keep going back to Arden she didn't understand? Maybe it was the great sex they'd had last night or maybe there really was something about being his mate. She wished that he was here.

The back of her neck was itching and had been since Arden brought her home last night. They'd made love again upstairs, but he'd left early this morning, saying he had pack business to tend too. She was hoping he'd be there to support her and Jade today.

Oh well, she thought. Maybe she was asking for too much. Finley walked over and put his arm around her. "The store looks wonderful, Quinn. From the crowd growing outside, I think it's going to be a success. Thanks for letting me work here until I can get back on my feet, and for just being here for someone to talk to." She understood Finley's fears, because she had the same ones. He lived at the pack house, and everyone had opened their arms up to him, but her being a witch had left most of the pack ignoring her. At least that's what she thought, since none of them have been by the store to say hello. Finley told her about pack members stopping by the house introducing themselves to him and bringing him cookies and other food items, but no one had come out to see her, even though she knew most of them had been to town. She couldn't think about it now, though—she had a living to make.

"Well, we're in this together, right? Plus, who else understands better than me? We were re-born on the same night, with that great big moon in the sky."

Quinn hugged Finley. "I'm glad you're my friend, too." She didn't want to start crying, so she let him go and walked away, brushing the tear away before anyone could see it. She'd never had true friends before, and what Finley said touched her deeply. She glanced back at everyone before she unlocked the door and turned the 'Open' sign on. "Everyone ready?"

"Ready," they all echoed back.

She smiled, plugged the sign in, and unlocked the door. Before she could open the door, though, it was being pulled from the outside. She backed up and welcomed everyone as they started piling inside. As she inhaled, she could already smell the coffeemakers brewing all kinds of coffee. Jade and her friends did a great job in getting the equipment there in one day, and working too. They didn't have many books yet, but Paley had found a bookstore going out of business in Atlanta and she immediately called and asked how much she wanted for her supplies. The lady didn't have much left, but they were all new books, so off she went with the others to pick up the coffeemakers and books. These kids were a godsend, and she couldn't thank them enough.

"Hello." Quinn opened her eyes to see Arden smiling back at her. He was holding a bouquet of wildflowers. "I thought these would look great over on the counter with all the different-colored candles."

"They're beautiful, Arden." Quinn murmured as she held the flowers to her nose.

"You're beautiful; these will do." Arden smiled. "It looks like opening day is a big success! While I waited outside for you to open, I could see even more vehicles pulling up."

"Thank you, Arden. I hope so, but I tell you, the ones who are going to be successful are those four back there. They've been wonderful to me. And I haven't told her yet, but Jade has sold three hundred purses online alone. She'll need some help in sewing her product, because she won't be able to do it by herself. I can't wait to tell her. I hope she has some friends who can sew."

"Are you kidding? There are a lot of people in the pack who can and are looking for work. The pack keeps them up because they can't find any jobs here, but they do odd jobs for people in the community. When are you going to tell her?"

"Let's go tell her now. I can't keep this in much longer." Quinn clapped her hands together, excited to give her the news.

Quinn and Arden walked over to the counter, where Jade was helping a lady pick out some bracelets for wedding gifts. Once she was done, Quinn couldn't hold it in any longer.

"Jade, I have some great news. I checked the computer before we opened, and you've already sold three hundred purses online. Do you realize what that means?" Jade looked stunned and speechless. "That means you're going to be a success, girl, and make great money! You need to hire some people to help you sew girl. You have a lot of orders to fill."

"I don't know what to say." Jade had tears in her eyes. "For so long, people have told me that I wouldn't amount to anything, and it kinda stuck inside me."

"Who told you that, sweetheart?" Arden demanded. He had his arm around her as the tears fell.

"Nobody, Alpha. I don't won't to drag anyone into this happy moment. I sold three hundred purses?"

Quinn smiled and nodded her head. "Yes ma'am, you did, and that means you need to hire some people to help you. We need to hire you an attorney, too, to make sure your line is protected and nobody can take it from you. The lawyer here in town drew up my papers, I'm sure it would be easy for him to do that for you. Plus, you have the money now."

"Miss, can you show me something?" A lady pointed at the jewelry cabinet.

"Of course," Jade answered, then told Quinn, "I'll get with you later."

They watched as she practically skipped over to the next counter.

"Look how happy she is." Quinn smiled.

"You did that for her, Quinn. I'm so ashamed that I didn't know people were filling her head with nonsense. She's a beautiful girl, who's going to be a big success. I could pound the ones who told her that."

"Well, look no further." Quinn nodded in the direction of the door, where Alice and two other girls had just walked in.

"I dealt with them today. Let me know if they cause any trouble? I called her out today at a pack meeting about how she lied to you. I had enough of it. I hope you believe me, Quinn. I haven't been with a soul since I met you, and I never will. I know you might not feel it yet, but you're it for me."

"Can you get me one of those pocket books down, sir?" Arden and Quinn both looked over at a young girl. She was pointing at one of Jade's purses, which was hanging on the wall.

"Of course. Which one would you like?" Arden asked. He was tall enough to reach the one she was pointing at.

"How much is it?" the girl asked.

"Well, this one is…" Arden looked at the tag. "This one is fifty-two dollars."

The girl smiled. "Thank you."

"You're welcome." Arden and Quinn watched the little girl take the pocketbook over to her mom.

"I think I'll stick around for a while and get purses off the wall," Arden said with a smile.

"That sounds great." Quinn walked over to the counters where Paley and Rick were feverishly ringing people up. She got behind the counter and started helping by putting their items in bags for them. The line started moving faster when she did.

When she looked up next it was already six at night, and the store was almost ready to close. Everyone looked tired, and when she examined the store most of her inventory had been sold. That meant she needed to get on the phone and order more, so that when they opened back up on Tuesday she would be re-stocked.

Quinn rushed over and locked the door after the last woman left. "We did it!" she yelled out. When she turned around everyone was smiling and coming up to congratulate her.

"This calls for a celebration," Jade announced. "Let's have a cook-out. What do you say, Quinn?"

"Um, well, I have a lot…"

"That can wait until tomorrow," Jade interrupted. "Finley can drive you out and maybe one of the guards can drive you back."

"Or I can." Quinn jerked her head in the direction of the voice. Her ears had to be deceiving her. But no, there was her brother smiling at her. She ran over to him and jumped in his arms. August was her twin, and he had red hair, too, but it was dark auburn rather than flame-red. He'd grown a goatee since she last saw him, and cut his hair short. He looked great; and normal, for once. He had on dark-colored blue jeans and a button-down shirt. Not the normal suit and tie she was used to him wearing as a successful doctor.

"When did you get here?" Quinn asked, excited to see her twin.

"A little while ago. I just watched to see how it was going, and it looked like you were selling a lot of stuff, Sister," August said proudly.

"Come here and meet the gang." Quinn pulled her reluctant brother over to Jade and her friends. "Everyone, this is my twin brother, August. He just surprised me with a visit, can he come too?"

"Of course he can," Jade answered immediately.

"Hey, can I talk to you in private?" Quinn narrowed her eyes at her brother for being so rude. He wasn't even acknowledging Jade or the others, and she wouldn't have any of that.

"Excuse us. Jade, give us thirty minutes and I can drive to the property." Quinn grabbed hold of her brother's hand and pulled him away toward the back door. A guard was standing at her stairs, and eyed her hand on her brother like she was up to something.

"Pete, this is my brother August. We'll be down in a few minutes, and then we've been invited to a cook-out behind the pack house with Jade and her friends." She could see Pete immediately relax when she told him that August was her brother. Unfortunately, she also knew that Pete would be calling the Alpha and telling him that August was here. He was a wizard, and that would mean two magic users on Dixon Land. She wondered if the pack would collapse in fear from them being so near, or if they would act like nothing was wrong. Because he was her brother, and nobody was going to tell her that he couldn't visit.

"What are you doing here, August?"

"Well, I'm happy to see you too, Sister," August said smartly.

"Look I know when you're lying, and I know something is up. What is it? Is something wrong at home?"

"Of course not, except that you're not there like you should be. But you don't need to be here, Quinn. You're too good for this hick town. Dad said if you come home now, he may be able to make sure our name isn't tarnished."

Quinn stared, then burst out laughing. "Did he make you learn that speech, or did you make that shit up yourself?"

August frowned. "You can't make me believe that this is what you want. In this hick town? You know you can open your own store back home where it's not so country. We're not like the wolves." Quinn was ashamed of how her brother was acting, sticking his nose up in the air like they were better than Jade and the rest of her pack. *Wow*, she thought, *I just called it my pack*. She smiled.

"What's so funny?"

"You are. I can't believe my own brother has his nose up in the air, just like our father. We've always despised that act. These people have shown me nothing but kindness—more than I ever got back home, August. I was going to tell you later, but I guess this is the best time to do it. I *am* just like the wolves. In fact, I'm a werewolf too."

August narrowed his eyes, then looked at her again. This time she could tell he could see the difference in her. "What happened to you?"

"Earlier this week I was attacked by a rogue wolf and turned. Ta-da." Quinn threw her hands up in the air.

"I'm going to fucking kill them. All of them." Quinn could see the magic storming around August.

She put her hands on his shoulder, stopping him. "Calm down. It was a rogue wolf, August, not this pack. But they did take me in, and they've helped me. I'm happy here. For the first time ever, I've found a place that I can call home and be happy in. Please don't ruin that, or try to make me go back to that hellhole."

Quinn watched all kinds of emotions run across August's face. "I'm happy here, and finally free of him. I make my own decisions, and my dreams of owning my own business have come true." She pulled him closer and whispered, "Please be happy for me; and August, you can leave too. You could be whatever you want here, and practice medicine too."

"Sister, you know I can't. He'll be…" August's voice stopped. She could see the stress he was under.

"Enough, August. We've been under his control long enough. I'm done, and you are too. You can practice anywhere. We don't need his approval." Quinn pulled her brother closer. "It's our time now. He had his chance, and if he wants to take over the Council then that's on him. But he isn't taking us with him when he fails; and make no mistake, brother, he will fail."

They both jerked when someone knocked on the door. Quinn dropped her hands. "Come in."

Finley had to duck as he came through the door. August looked up at him in surprise. She thought he'd left already.

"Hey. Finley, I want you to meet my brother, August."

Finley walked forward with a smile on his face and stuck out his hand. August was still looking up at him when Quinn elbowed him in the side. Finally, he took Finley's hand and shook it. "I wanted to see if you needed a ride to the property."

"I think I'll just drive and follow you. That way you don't have to come back here," Quinn told him.

"Okay, well if you're ready the store is locked up and all the lights are off. Jade called and said they had the steaks on the grill." Finley said over his shoulder as he walked out the door.

*****

"Nice property," August muttered as they walked over to the back of the pack house. Jade and the others already had the picnic tables set up, and food was coming off the grill.

"Great timing." Jade announced as she put the last steak on the plate. "Come on, sit down." Quinn, August, and Finley sat down with Jade.

Quinn wondered where Arden was, but didn't say anything. Right now her brother was in town and she wanted him to like it here and stay.

The group asked August a lot of questions as they ate dinner. He mellowed out some and was actually nice and acted like he was having a good time. She wanted her brother here with her.

"Let's go and sit by the fire." Jade suggested. It was a cool night, and it felt good to relax by the bonfire, but of course Alice and her group of minions showed up to spoil it. She was mad about something, Quinn could tell, and she was ready for a fight.

"You found some friends that actually want to be around you, huh Scarface?" Alice said, and just like the mean girls in the movies, all her friends laughed along with her. When she looked over at Jade, she could tell she was finally getting mad.

"Shut up!" Quinn shouted. She couldn't and wouldn't take anymore of her cruelness. Alice's head whipped around.

"What're you going to do about it, witch?"

"You really don't want to mess with me, Alice. I'm not going to sit here and just take your shit." Quinn could hear someone coming out the door, but she didn't turn around for fear of Alice jumping on her when her back was turned.

"I challenge you, witch." Alice stood proudly as she said it.

Quinn moved around the fire pit and saw that it was Bane and Arden who'd come out. *Of course he shows up now.* It didn't matter—she wasn't taking any shit from anyone anymore. "I don't know what a challenge means, but if it means me whipping your ass then I'm in."

Quinn looked over at Bane, who nodded at her. She hoped the lessons he'd given her would pay off. They'd only worked on it a couple of times, but she had some other training she could use, too. All her life she'd been taught how to defend herself. Tonight she was going to put it all together and use it against Alice.

"Quinn, what are you doing?" August tried to talk to her, but she didn't have time to explain before they both started taking their clothes off. "Stop this, Quinn."

Quinn shifted along with Alice, and she was faster. She didn't waste any time before she leaped on Alice, scraping her claws down her back before she was thrown off. Alice was stronger than she'd expected, but she wasn't giving up. She watched as Alice gave away her tells, signaling when she was going to do something. Her father drilled it into her head that people were predictable, and that she just had to wait for that right moment.

She saw the sign she was looking for, and before Alice could move she was on top of her and had her jaws wrapped around Alice's neck. Squeezing her jaws together, Quinn could taste the blood of defeat as Alice whimpered. But before she could give up, Quinn was floating through the air, landing behind her brother. Shit, he did the one thing that he shouldn't have done—use magic.

As she shifted back, she could hear Arden yelling at August. All the wolves had backed up behind their Alpha. They were scared. August had his hands up, chanting a protection spell. She jumped up and ran to her brother.

"Stop, August. Stop! I'm not hurt. You're scaring them. Stop." Quinn grabbed her brother, pulling him back.

"See, I told you, they're bad people. He's probably cast a spell on all of us!" Alice yelled out, bringing more pack members out of the house.

"Get off my property," Arden demanded, and pointing toward August. She could see the veins in his neck standing out, and knew he was almost to the point of shifting. He would kill August. And now she had her answer; he wasn't her mate. She'd thought she was falling in love and that he was in love with her, but she was wrong.

She pulled August over to her pile of clothes and put them on. Jade tried to go over to her, but Arden yelled again, "No, Jade."

Quinn looked over at him. He hated who she was and what she represented, and it would never work. She hoped that she could find another place to go open her store where there weren't paranormal people of any kind. She had to keep looking, because she would never go back to her father.

"Let's go, August. I'm done here," Quinn spit out. She had to leave before she started crying. She wouldn't let the man see her cry.

Finley walked over to her, stopping her before she left. "Quinn, I'm sorry. I don't know what to do to fix this."

She put her hand up to his face. "It's okay, Fin. It's best that I leave this area anyway. They fear my kind, and he can't accept me either. It won't hurt so bad if I don't have to see him anymore."

"Then I'm leaving too. If they can't accept you then I'm not going to be part of his bigoted pack."

"Quinn, what the hell is going on?" August pleaded.

"I'll explain in the car." Quinn smiled sadly and dropped her hand. "Fin, I can't ask you to leave. You fit in here. Apparently I don't, and never will, just because I'm a witch."

Chapter 11

"Quinn?" August said her name bringing her out of her thoughts. They'd been driving in silence up till then.

She just blurted it out. "Arden is the Alpha of the Dixon pack, and when he was a child, a witch cursed his father with a spell. She was angry because his father wouldn't turn her daughter, and the daughter killed herself. In revenge, she cast a spell that would make his father shift and kill his son, but Arden's mother got in his way before he could, and he killed her."

"The pack got to his father before he could kill Arden, but the Death Hunters were sent out and they killed both the witch and Arden's father. The pack fears any witch, and until me there hadn't been one in New Hope for over thirty years." She glanced over at her brother before she dropped the biggest bomb. "I'm the Alpha's mate, August."

"Oh God, please tell me you're joking?"

"Nope. I'm in love with him, but him acting like this toward us just proved to me that I can't be with someone who hates me because I'm a witch. I was born this way, just like he was born a wolf. It's who I am. He can't take that, and I'm done trying. I just wanted to find a place to fit in, and now that's gone." Quinn gripped the steering wheel harder. He'd chosen Alice over her. He had to see that Alice was the one starting the fight.

Of course, she was a half-breed. Just thinking that made her sick to her stomach. She had to pack the store up, and just find a place to live and concentrate on her online store instead. That way she couldn't offend anyone. Fuck, she couldn't stand what she was saying to herself.

Right now she was sick over all of this, and thinking about it was killing her. Her wolf was angry as well; she could feel it inside of her.

*****

Arden watched as Quinn, Finley, and her brother left. He couldn't control his anger anymore and wanted to unleash it on Bane. "She's *my* mate, so why are you and Quinn looking at each other?"

"Maybe you should have a little faith in your mate and stop trying to control who she is…" Before Bane could say anything further, Arden hit him in the face, and the fight was on. Arden finally looked up to find two men standing to the side watching him and Bane fight. That's when Bane hit him with a right hook, knocking him to the ground. He shook his head, trying to clear the stars from his eyes.

"Good lick," Arden muttered. When he looked up, Bane was holding his hand down to help him get up.

"You're still an ass. You should know better than to think that something is going on between me and your mate," Bane scolded. They both looked over at the two men standing beside a frowning Tate. "Who are they?"

Arden wasn't in the mood, but he knew who these men were. "Death Hunters' attitudes are always the same. Cocky and arrogant, and the fact that they have swords strapped to their backs just gives it away."

Bane laughed. "Dude, you just described yourself, apart from the sword."

Arden walked over to the men. "Why can't you let us deal with this?"

The little one smirked, but the big fucker was obviously in charge.

"The Council sent us to help find the rogues," he said.

"I explained to the Council that we could handle it." Arden narrowed his eyes at the man. He didn't like them already.

"So you've found them?" The smaller one asked.

"No, asshole, we haven't," Bane countered.

"Then it looks like we're going to be helping you with that little problem," the larger one continued.

"Do we call you Death Hunters, or do you want to give us your names?" Arden asked.

"I'm Lennox Bartley, and my Beta is Cosmo Fitzgerald."

Arden inhaled. He could feel the tension among his guards. He needed to get this situation under control before something worse happened.

"Tate." His cousin frowned at the two men, then looked over at his Alpha. "Find the Death Hunters a place to sleep. The two rooms open in our part of the house are fine."

Arden already knew that they would send someone, so Bane already had the rooms ready. They watched as Tate took the Death Hunters to get settled.

"What do you think they really want?" Bane asked.

"To wipe the pack off the face of the earth, including the women and children," Arden said, still watching as they left.

"I'll have a problem with that," Bane replied.

"Alert the pack, and let's keep a watch on them," Arden said, then turned toward Bane. "What was up with the looks you and Quinn were giving each other?" He didn't want any shit from his Beta; he wanted to know what was going on.

"Alice came into the store the other day starting her shit, and I told Quinn that eventually Alice would challenge her in wolf form. She told me that she knew how to fight in human form, but had no idea what to do in wolf form, and I said that I could train her. Our Alpha female needs to know how to kick ass, and she's good, Arden. Really good."

"Why didn't you tell me?"

"Because she told me not to, and she's my Alpha too. I wanted her to succeed in kicking Alice's ass," Bane said.

At first Arden smiled, then he couldn't hold it in any longer and started laughing. "You're such an idiot." He leaned over, putting his hands on his knees. "I screwed up, didn't I?"

"Yep. Again," Bane agreed.

*****

Quinn and August pulled up at the back of her apartment, and she noticed that the back door was standing wide open. "Shit, someone broke into the store." She dialed 911, and it went straight to the police station. While she was giving the information to the dispatcher, Finley pulled up behind her.

He got out and looked around. She and August got out of the car. "Did you call the police?"

"Yes," Quinn answered. "Do you smell that?" It smelled like rotten eggs.

"It smells like someone egged the place," August answered. She could see how his magic was circling him. Her brother was a powerful wizard, and he could cast a spell faster than anyone she knew. He was preparing his magic for defensive casts.

The chief pulled up and got out with his gun drawn. Another police car also pulled up. "Stay here while we check the store out," Deaton said.

They all waited, but Quinn knew something was wrong inside. She could tell that this was going to make her so mad. Finally, the chief came out, rubbing his head. He looked at her with pity on his face.

"I'm sorry Quinn, but the store is destroyed. They tore everything up and it smells like rotten eggs and piss inside."

Quinn didn't wait; she pushed the chief aside and ran into the store. The lights were on, but the sight of her store made her physically sick. All the counters were kicked in, and the glass was broken. They'd taken a knife and cut up all the clothes and purses—what was left of them.

Most of the store inventory had been sold earlier, but the rest was completely destroyed.

Her brother and Finley came to stand beside her. August put his hand on her shoulder, but she pushed it off and went back outside. She didn't say anything to anyone, just walked up the stairs to her apartment. At least her apartment was still intact. She unlocked the door, went inside, and headed straight to the bathroom. She locked the door behind her and turned on the tub faucets.

It was all gone. All the inventory she had left, and all the money she'd spent on the books, coffeemakers, and counters. They'd even drawn a special message on the wall for her: "I'm coming for you." Right now she was so mad that she was going to start throwing magic at anything and everything, and she couldn't do that. All she wanted to do was sink under the water and cry her eyes out. Cry for losing the one she loved, cry for losing her friends, and cry for losing her store. She'd lost everything, all in one day. She turned off the water and sat down in the tub, then leaned back into the hot water. Once she got comfortable, she let go of all the emotions she had bottled up. She held the washcloth against her mouth and sobbed.

*****

August walked upstairs after he gave the police all of his sister's information. Finley was with him, and when they heard her in the bathroom crying, August almost lost it. She'd looked so happy when he arrived and now someone had done this to her. Why?

Finley put his hand on August's shoulder. "Your sister needs you now. We can get our revenge later, but right now she's hurting, and I think it's mostly about the Alpha."

"No, I don't think so, especially after how he acted earlier. She couldn't love him, and let's be honest—the way he treated her, he doesn't deserve her." August went over to the door and knocked lightly. "Quinn, come on out, sweetheart."

"I just need some time alone. I'll be out later." Quinn's voice was low and defeated.

August shook his head and walked over to Finley. "Give me that asshole's number." Finley looked at him for a minute, then took his phone out and repeated the number to him. August punched the number in and went outside.

Arden answered on the second ring. "How is she?" That's what the asshole had the audacity to ask.

"She is a wreck, you son of a bitch. You've destroyed my sister and the love she had for you, and that fucking rogue pack destroyed her store. She has nothing now." August thought he heard a click, and when he pulled his phone away from his ear he saw the fucker had hung up on him.

August walked back in the room and glanced up at Finley. "The arrogant son of a bitch hung up on me. That's fine; she's too good for him anyway and I'll take her somewhere else where she can be herself and open her store up and enjoy life. We…" Finley looked up at him, and he sighed. "We didn't have a great childhood with our father. He took away any control we had, and made life miserable for us. Quinn got away, and today I actually saw her happy for the first time in a very long time. Now that asshole has broken her heart, and that damn pack needs to be wiped off the face of the earth. If I find them first, I'll make it happen. I can promise you that." August walked out the door, leaving Finley inside. He needed a moment to get his thoughts together. All he wanted to do was rain fire down into the woods and hope they were laying there watching.

August was sitting on the steps, trying to calm down, when three vehicles pulled up. He waited to see who it was, and when he saw the man responsible for his sister's heartache, he bolted down the stairs. "You need to leave, you bastard."

The rage he was feeling was so close to the surface that he wanted to explode.

Finley came up behind him and put his hand on his shoulder. "Now isn't the time. Looks like he brought help."

August never wanted to hit somebody so badly before; except his father, but that was another story. He glanced back at Finley in shock, but his attention was over his shoulder. Turning around, his eyes located the biggest men he had ever seen.

The big man and one other walked over and inhaled, then continued to the store's door and went inside. Arden and Bane followed them. August walked in behind them and watched as the two men walked around the store inspecting the mess.

"Who are they?" August asked.

"Death Hunters," Arden answered as he continued to watch the strangers.

"You brought fucking Death Hunters to my sister's store?" August ran his fingers through his hair. "You're crazy. I've got to take my sister away from all of you crazy people."

"She's not going anywhere. She's my mate." Arden didn't even look at him when he said it. Like he was sure his commands would be followed. This was hitting too close to home for August, and he knew what Quinn would do if she heard him.

"Well, watch me." August turned around and walked outside. He'd started up the stairs when Arden put his hand out and stopped him.

"I love your sister."

"You have a funny way of showing it." August had had enough of this man and his arrogant ways. Before he could get his anger under control, he turned and punched Arden in the face, knocking him backwards. He knew he hit him hard, but the wolf's face felt like granite.

"I'll let you have that one, but not again. I fucked up and I know it, but I love her and she's my mate. I should've stood up for her today, but the magic..."

"Scares you. Yeah, she told me. We're not like that witch. She was bad from the start, and we don't use the Craft for revenge. You can't judge us all because of one bad witch, and you can't keep putting my sister on the back burner while you mess with her head. She's been through too much growing up with my father. Come on man, you've treated her like shit. Don't you see that?"

"I just need to talk to her and explain."

"Just so you know if she leaves I leave, and if she stays I stay. So you need to make up your mind before you talk to her whether you can stand a family of witches in your town—and, if she's really your mate, in your pack. I'm not leaving my sister again. Frankly, I don't think you can take care of her." August turned around, then muttered, "She's not even talking to me, and that's unusual. Maybe you should come back tomorrow, let her calm down tonight. She doesn't trust you anymore, and trust is important to her," he explained, and walked back up the stairs. "I can't believe I'm even talking to you."

He locked the door and went over to the bathroom again, but didn't hear Quinn crying anymore. He didn't hear anything, in fact, and that scared him. He used some of his magic to unlock the door, and when he walked in, Quinn was still in the tub, fast asleep.

Apparently, nudity was nothing to wolves, but this was his sister. He hated picking her up while she was naked, but she could drown if he didn't. He shook his head, got a towel out and laid it on the floor, then closed his eyes and reached in the tub. He picked his sister up, laid her on the towel, and covered her up. Then he carried her into her bedroom and put her to bed. He was going to take the couch in case the rogues came back, because if they did they would get a lot of fire.

Chapter 12

Quinn woke up to the smell of bacon frying. Since she'd been turned, she loved meat and more meat. She was starving and she knew she needed the energy to tackle the clean-up she had waiting downstairs. But she'd made a decision; she wasn't leaving town. She wouldn't go back on pack land, but she wasn't giving up her store and what she had in it. She could get more inventories, and she could put spells around the store so the rogues couldn't get back in, but she wasn't going to let anyone run her off. *Screw them,* she thought, then got up and took a shower.

When she walked out into the living room, Finley and August were talking and cooking. "Good morning."

She smiled and kissed her brother on the cheek, then kissed Finley too. They both watched her as she poured herself a cup of coffee. She added an extra shot each of chocolate and vanilla. She was going to need it.

"How are you feeling this morning?" August asked. She could see the concern on his face as she sipped from her cup.

"Actually, pretty good. I needed the sleep and I need to eat." Quinn grabbed a piece of bacon and put it in her mouth. "And I've made some decisions, too."

"Does it include us packing you up and leaving here forever?" August said with a smirk.

"Nope. But I'm not going to be part of the pack, and I will not go onto their land. And I'm not closing my store. Once it's cleaned up I'll do some spells around the store and apartment to make sure they can't come back. If any of those bitches mess with me again, I'll kick their asses both in wolf form and as a witch. So, brother, if that isn't the answer you're looking for, cry about it." Quinn smiled, then started piling food on her plate.

Finley finally broke the silence that followed her declaration. "What do you need to start the cleaning process? I'll go and get the supplies from the store."

"That would be great, Fin. Thanks for helping me out, and for sticking by me. I know that you were friends with everyone there."

"Look Quinn, I'm not one of those people who are going to be mad about something that happened thirty years ago. Nothing is wrong with you, and if they can't see that then I don't want to be part of their pack. We came in this world bitten on the same day, and we need to stick together."

Quinn felt the tears gathering in her eyes. "Thank you, Finley. I don't have many friends, and I would really like to keep you as one."

"You got it." Finley popped some bacon in his mouth and got up from the table. "I'm off for some cleaning supplies. Text me if you need something special."

Quinn nodded and watched her friend walk out the door.

"He's a good guy," August commented.

"Yeah, he is." Quinn finished her food, then put her plate in the dishwasher. "Now I need to start the clean-up." August opened the door and they walked down the stairs together. Both of them stopped at the bottom when they heard something inside the store. August chanted a protection spell, which surrounded them as he jerked the door open.

Both stood and gawked at the Dixon pack cleaning up the store. They already had most of it fixed, and some of the men were making another counter and painting. Arden walked over and stood beside her. "I think we got most of it cleaned up, but we need to build another counter for the jewelry and buy another coffee thingy."

"Coffee thingy?" Quinn asked, confused.

"Yeah, that machine that makes those different flavors of coffee," Arden said with a smirk.

"Hmm. We'll have to order that." Quinn didn't want him being nice to her now. She was still mad at him for being a complete ass, and she was getting tired of it. "I'm shocked that you're fraternizing with the enemy."

"What do you mean?"

"You know, seeing that I'm a witch and all." Quinn glared at Arden as she said it.

"Quinn, I need to apologize to you. I'm sorry. I wish I'd handled that differently, but I didn't. I made a complete fool of myself."

"Wow, at least you can admit it," August contributed.

Arden frowned at her brother, then pulled Quinn over to the side. "Look, I wish I could take back what happened. I hope we can start over and—" Quinn turned around to see what had gotten Arden's attention. Two of the biggest men she'd ever seen were walking toward them. Arden pulled her closer to him as they stopped in front of her.

"You're Quinn?" The bigger of the two asked.

She gave him a once-over before she answered. "Yes, and you are?"

"My name is Lennox Bartley, and this is my Beta Cosmo Fitzgerald."

"Death Hunters," Quinn stated flatly. Arden narrowed his eyes as he looked over at her.

"Yes. We're here to find the rogues and take care of them. I have some questions, if you wouldn't mind?" Lennox asked.

"Sure, why not." Lennox and Quinn moved over to a table that had made it through the trashing.

"Absolutely beautiful," Cosmo muttered as he watched them walk off.

Arden turned to Cosmo. "You fucking touch her and I will kill you. She's my mate."

Narrowing his eyes at him, the Death Hunter looked over at Quinn again. "Don't see a mark yet."

"She was just turned, and I was giving her time," Arden answered.

"Hmm." Cosmo looked thoughtful, then walked over and sat down at the table with Lennox and Quinn.

"If I were you I would get over there with her," August said, shaking his head.

*****

Arden walked over to the table and listened.

"Do you feel any connection to the wolf that bit you?" Lennox was asking.

"What the hell? No, she doesn't feel anything for him," Arden answered for her.

"Dammit Arden, I think I'm old enough to answer for myself." Quinn got up from the table. "No, I don't feel a damn thing for the wolf," she said, staring at Arden, and then walked off.

"Looks like your mate wants you real bad," Cosmo said with a smirk.

"If you want to keep your head then I advise that when it comes to her you back the fuck off." Arden said.

*****

Jade ran up to Quinn and hugged her. "I'm sorry about last night. I should've known that Alice would start something when she saw you there. I hope we can still be friends?"

"Of course we can, Jade. I just thought maybe somebody would have had my back last night and took up for me."

Jade lowered her head in shame. "I know. I hope you can forgive me." Quinn watched as she moved away.

There was still a lot for them to do, but if the store was going to be a success she needed to find another one of those 'coffee thingys.' She smiled as she went back to her office to make a call.

After about a half an hour, she finally found one, and they were willing to hold it for her, too. She punched the air in triumph. When she went back out into the store, it looked like new again. They were still putting together some counters and tables, but the smell was gone, and the graffiti, too.

Arden walked over to her and pulled her back into the office. "I've got to go back to the house with them, but I want you home with me. That's where you belong."

Quinn narrowed her eyes at the Alpha for thinking she was going to do exactly what he said. She snorted. "Where do you get off on thinking that I'm ever going back to that property again? I'm a witch, Arden."

"I know you are, Quinn. I'll say it this way then: you'll be back at our house tonight, or I promise you I'll hunt your pretty ass down and take you myself." Arden bent down and nipped her lip. When she gasped he found his opportunity and kissed her deeply, leaning her backwards until she couldn't stop kissing him back. He tasted like the mints she had sitting on one of the tables. He wasn't going to get off this easy in thinking that he could control her, the bastard. She pushed him back until he let her go.

"Tonight, Quinn," he muttered, then walked out the door with the Death Hunters.

"Cocky, arrogant, big-headed wolf," Quinn grumbled out loud.

"Quinn," Jade whispered. "Are you okay?"

She couldn't stay mad at Jade. She was a good woman, and like everyone, just needed to work on taking up for herself.

"Yeah, I'm fine." Quinn grabbed her purse and inched her way toward the door as she watched all the guards help Finley put the counter back together.

"Where are you going?" Jade asked watching her sidle backwards.

"Be quiet. I want to go get another coffee machine. They're holding it for me, and if I don't go get it then they'll sell it to someone else. I'm not taking the guards with me, either. I don't need them." Quinn whispered as she stepped backwards again, closer to the door.

"Then I'm going with you." Jade grabbed her hand and they quietly made their way to the door. As soon as they stepped outside, Quinn felt the wind as a fist connected with her face. Before the lights went out, she thought of Arden.

Chapter 13

It was the smell of rotten eggs that woke her. Slowly she tried to open her eyes, but the pain in her head was throbbing. She finally managed to force them open, and blinked for a bit. When she tried to touch her face, where the pain was coming from, she couldn't.

Cursing her very existence, Quinn looked up and saw that her hands were tied together. Bits and pieces of what happened started to wander into her memory as she looked around. The smell was ungodly, and she tried to breathe out of her mouth. Now she knew where that smell was coming from, but what she didn't know was where she was at. When she turned her head to the other side she saw Jade tied up the same way, but she was still out cold.

"Jade! Jade, wake up. Jade," she said it with a little more purpose, trying to get her attention before someone walked in. Finally Jade's eyes sprang open. They were yellow as her wolf peered through. Quinn hadn't been a wolf very long, but if she was a betting woman, she'd say Jade's wolf was making sure she was safe.

"Quinn?" Jade's voice was groggy from being knocked out.

"Be quiet. I don't know where we're at or who took us," Quinn explained, trying to keep her voice low.

Jade looked around and shook her head. "We're in the old mines outside of town. I knew I recognized that scent from somewhere. This mine has been closed for over fifty years."

She moved her head so her arm would push against her nose, blocking the airflow. "God, what is that smell?" Quinn asked.

"It's sulphur coming up from the mine. This is an old coal mine. It caved in and they couldn't use it anymore. Too unstable. Plus, the gases that came out of this place smelled like—"

"Rotten eggs," both of them said at the same time.

"Shit, now all the rocks are going to cave in on us," Quinn said, still looking around. Then it hit her. *You're a witch, so get yourself untied.* Settling her thoughts, Quinn repeated an unbinding spell, but when she looked up at the handcuffs holding her hostage, nothing had happened.

"I can't use my magic," Quinn muttered, then tried the spell over again.

"Of course you can't, you fool." Quinn looked in front of her as a woman and a man she'd never seen before walked toward her. She could tell the man had been the wolf who bit her. He was the rogue Alpha they'd been talking about.

"Hello Quinn. I'm your maker—and mate," the man said, with a smile on his face that was pure evil. She could feel a cold chill slide down her backbone as he got closer. He was covered in black smut, and his hair was oily and greasy-looking. She wanted to point out that there was a pond right there he could bathe himself in, but clearly they needed to look the part.

"You're not my mate, and you're not my maker. You may have bitten me, but you don't control me." She had to stay strong; she couldn't let him sense any weakness.

"Ah, your first fight." The woman said with a smirk, and Quinn thought this one was crazier than he was. Lord, didn't these people have a mirror to look in, or someone to say, 'hey, you might want to get the black coal off your face and clothes.' Then again, she clearly wasn't dealing with people who had a full deck.

"Who are you people?" she asked, trying to show confidence.

"Well, I'm going to be your sister-in-law, Hannah Hoffman."

"Lady you're about a dollar short and completely out of your mind if you think anything like that is going to happen," Quinn answered.

"So how do you like your new home?" Silas smirked.

"I think I want my money back."

"We didn't all grow up with a silver spoon in our mouth. Be careful or you will be buried here," Hannah answered.

"Quinn, this is your future sister-in-law, and she's a witch just like you," Silas informed her, patting his sister on the shoulder.

"Well, let's cut to the chase then. I don't plan on being in this family, but why have you kidnapped us?" Quinn was losing patience with this mangy mutt.

"Glad you asked. Our sister was Beatrice Hoffman," Silas explained, like the name should mean something to her. Quinn looked around, then back at them, confused.

"The witch who cast the spell on Arden's dad," Jade filled in.

"Yes, our beloved sister was killed because of Arden Dixon's father, and now he will pay for his father's sins," Silas vowed.

Quinn twisted to look behind her again. When she looked back at Silas and Hannah, Silas asked, "What are you doing?"

"Looking for the cameras. I think I'm in the wrong movie. You know, the mafia movies where the bad guy says, 'Now you'll pay for your father's sins.'" Quinn smiled, and Hannah slapped her in the mouth.

Quinn screamed out and kicked her legs forward, trying to hit Hannah. "You bitch. I'll pay you back for that, you mangy, rotten-egg smelling cunt."

Hannah lunged toward her, but Silas jerked her backwards. "Don't touch my mate again. Enough!" Silas grabbed Quinn's head and jerked her close to his face. "You smell ripe, like I could eat you up. Soon you'll be mine, and when you are I'll teach you your first lesson—to watch your mouth." Silas licked her face, then pulled her shirt off her shoulder. "Now what do we have here? I don't see any mating marks. Oh my, what a shame."

"Let me go." Quinn tried to jerk away, but Silas pushed her, watching as she swayed backwards.

"What do you want?" Jade yelled.

"I want the Alpha's head on a stick, and I'm going to get it." Silas smiled.

"You aren't strong enough, and he has a whole pack behind him. He probably knows exactly where you are right now," Jade sneered.

Silas and Hannah both laughed. "We know exactly what he's doing right now."

It dawned on both the girls what Silas was implying. "Nobody in the pack would betray their Alpha."

"Who says they're original pack members?" Hannah taunted Jade.

"Finley? How could you make Finley do that?" Quinn asked.

"Told you she was a smart one, Sister." Silas reached out to touch Quinn's face, but before he could she snarled and tried to bite his hand.

Jerking his hand back, Silas's eyes glazed over. "I love it when you fight." Then he grabbed a hold of her face, shoving it to the side and moving to bite her when Hannah pulled him back.

"No, Silas. It will make it so much better when he sees you mate with her. We have to wait. Let's go and set the spell in motion."

"What are you going to do?" Quinn demanded.

"Since you'll be family in a few, I'll go ahead and tell you. Your friend Finley is a spy for us. He doesn't even know that he's my puppet; my lap dog to do whatever I want with. We know what's been going on, especially with you. If Arden wanted you, then he should've mated with you. But lucky for us he is giving you time to adjust to being a wolf. How sweet and stupid. If he was a true Alpha then he would have taken you and mated with you whether you were adjusted or not."

"Why would Finley do that to us?" Jade whispered.

"He doesn't know he's doing it, stupid girl. He's under a spell. If you had a witch in your pack she could protect members of your pack with magic, but no, instead of being afraid of the big bad wolf, you're all afraid of a witch. Now look at you. Soon you all will be bound to us." Hannah grabbed Silas's hand. "Let's go, Silas, before we run out of time."

They both started walking out, but Hannah turned back. "Oh yeah, in case you want to use some of that magic, you can't. I put a protection marker on the cave. You can't do any magic in the cave. See you later, little sister." Hannah laughed.

Quinn waited for a soundtrack of pure doom to start playing, but nothing happened. She listened until she was sure they were gone, then said, "We have to get out of here and warn Arden. They're going to put a spell on him."

When Jade didn't say anything, Quinn whispered, "Jade are you okay?"

At first Jade was silent, then she turned and looked at her. "Something is bugging me."

Quinn laughed. "Well it's not like we don't have time to kill. What's bugging you?"

"Do you love him? Jade asked. "Because if you don't, and you don't feel the mating pull, then maybe when this is over you should leave. Because he'll only ever want you. He'll never want or have anyone else. I know you don't understand that right now, because you weren't born like this, but when we find our mate it's everything. Our world revolves around that person. I don't know if he'll survive if you leave, but being around you all the time when he can't have you will kill him too."

"Thanks, Jade. No pressure and all." Quinn took a deep breath, despite the smell. "You know, all my life, my dad has told me who I could like, hang out with, and even love. He told me when I was younger that I couldn't love my boyfriend, unless he said I could. Damn Jade, he was so controlling. I couldn't breathe anymore. Have you ever been so controlled that even what you ate could be held against you? I wish I could have grown up with a pack who took care of each other—well, we can take Alice out of that bunch—but all the others have been pretty great."

"You didn't answer my question. Do you love him?" Jade asked again.

Quinn sighed, "Yeah, I do. But it's the controlling part that I'm having a hard time with. I love him, but what if he starts to try and tell me what to do?"

"My dad told me the story of what happened when the witch cast the spell, and Arden's mom and dad were killed. My dad said that Arden was a complete mess. He was the Alpha's son, and then he wasn't anyone. Everything and everyone had been taken from him. He had no one, and my dad and family helped him and loved him, but you know he's always waiting for something or someone else to leave him. It scares him, Quinn, knowing you're his mate, and you're this close to becoming a family, but then he watches you slip right between his fingers. He holds on tight because he fears he'll lose you, just like his parents and the life he used to know. Just like that, it was taken from him. Hell that's hard for an adult to grasp, much less a kid. Maybe you could cut him some slack and understand that, just like you, he had a terrible childhood, and that's why he holds on too tight and tries to control you. He's scared, too."

Quinn listened to Jade and finally understood. He was holding on for fear of losing her.

"Also, when he is being too much, then tell him no, but do it in private. I think once this is over everything will work out," Jade finished, then looked around the room.

"If we ever get out of here," Quinn whispered.

"What?" Jade asked.

"I don't see how were going to get out of here if I can't use my magic. I don't know about you, but can you get out of silver handcuffs?" Quinn said, then pulled on the cuffs, making her skin burn.

Jade laughed. "Well we need to find a way to jump into the water then, because last I checked it wasn't part of the cave."

Quinn looked over at her, then at the water and back again. "What did you say?"

"What?"

"You're a freaking genius, Jade. That's it."

"What's it?"

"The water. Her spell. The water isn't part of the cave. I doubt she included it. And either way, if we can swim to the other side of it, which is definitely outside the cave, then I can use my magic." Quinn smiled as they both started laughing. Then Jade frowned.

"But...how are we going to get to the water?"

Chapter 14

Quinn closed her eyes to think. *What can we do to get out of here?* Right now all she wanted to do was puke from the smell.

"That's it." Quinn looked over at Jade and smiled. "I hope you can act, because you're going to have to pretend that you're dead. When he takes the cuffs off you, don't waste any time in shifting and going straight for that water."

"Help!" Quinn screamed. She glanced over at Jade, whose head was down like she was dead. "Please help us." Quinn could hear someone walking. She hung her head forward for added effect.

"What's going on in here?" She glanced up with weak eyes and whispered so he would come closer. "She's sick, please help her."

The guard looked at Jade, then unhooked her and took off one of the cuffs. Jade's head rolled back with her mouth open like she'd just died. "They don't care about her, just you." Then, he threw her down to the ground. Quinn wanted to say something about how careless he was with her body, but right now her plan was working.

"Help me," Quinn moaned, which quickly got the wolf's attention.

The wolf looked behind him, then smiled. "I've got something that will help you." Then he undid one of her handcuffs. She could see Jade already shifting when she brought her knee up, catching the guard in the nuts. When he bent over gasping, Quinn used the handcuff and hit him square in the head with it. She didn't know how long he would be down, but Jade was already in the water when she took off running. She tripped when the guard grabbed her leg, but she kicked him in the face and he let go. She got up and ran, diving into the water.

Sputtering as she came up on the other side, Quinn saw Jade fighting another guard. The man had a stick and was about to hit her with it when Quinn used her magic on him. Flicking her wrist, Quinn spun the man around in circles. He would keep twirling until she released him. She swam up to the side of the pond and dragged herself out. Jade was still in wolf form, and if they were going to get to Arden in time, they would have to run and run hard.

She couldn't hold the spell after she shifted, and the man would stop turning; but by the looks of him he wouldn't be able to do much until his head stopped spinning. In fact, there he went, throwing up all over himself as he spun. She shifted and followed Jade into the woods.

Her mate and the pack were in trouble, and if they didn't get there quick Hannah would use her magic on Arden. The Death Hunters were already there, and who knew what they would do to him if he hurt someone while under a spell.

*****

Finley knocked on the Pattersons' door. Peg and David Patterson were Elders in the pack, and both were born in the pack. Peg had brought cookies to him every day since he was turned. He really liked the Patterson's, but for the life of him he couldn't remember why he was knocking on their door.

David opened the door with a smile, and Finley hit the older man, knocking him out. He carried him to the back bedroom and laid him down on the bed. Peg walked into the room. "What happened?"

"Stay in here, Peg." Finley closed the door, then went to the back of the house and unlocked it for Silas and Hannah.

"Where are the old people?" Hannah asked.

"In the bedroom," Finley answered then followed Hannah into the bedroom, where Peg was holding her husband's head in her lap.

"You did so good, my pet." Hannah rubbed up and down Finley's arm.

"I know you're in there, Finley. Fight her." Peg's voice was soft as she encouraged him.

"Like he can really fight me, old woman," Hannah laughed.

"Witch, you have no control over me." Peg spit at Hannah, infuriating the witch. She reached back to hit Peg, but Finley grabbed her hand, stopping her, then pushed her away. Before Peg could say anything further, Finley tied her hands and feet and put some tape over her mouth so she couldn't yell out.

"Leave her alone," Finley's voice was harsh.

Hannah stared up into Finley's face, her black eyes hardening as she glanced back at the old couple. "Remember who controls you, my pet."

Hannah turned to walk away but stopped and glanced over her shoulder. "These old people won't be here much longer. We need warriors for our cause. You would be wise to remember that. Their time is almost up."

*****

Arden, Bane, August, and the pack guards had a table pulled out with papers scattered across it. "We need to check every house and property. I know they're still here. I feel it."

"What do they want?" Bane asked, tilting his head toward Lennox and Cosmo as they approached the table. "And what are those strapped to their backs?"

Arden knew exactly what they were. The Swords of Justice had been used to kill his father. He remembered everything that happened that day.

"Why do you have swords?" August asked.

Cosmo looked toward Lennox, who nodded, before he answered. "To kill people with." When nobody laughed at his joke, he shook his head. "They are the Swords of Justice."

"I thought they were a myth. Made-up stories, like the boogeyman," August said. He looked more closely at the blades. "Are they really made by Ozark and Phelmine?"

"Who are Ozark and Phelmine?" Bane asked.

"They were the most powerful witch and wizard known. They forged swords for a group of Hunters who would hunt down paranormals who could not be redeemed; the ones who were considered cruel and evil. I just never thought it was true, because we have never seen you guys," August said.

"Now you have." Lennox answered without any emotion. "And when we find the ones who are responsible for this, we'll do our job and kill them."

*****

Silas and Hannah watched out the window. "It's time to end this, Sister."

Hannah smiled and pointed toward Arden, speaking his name and then beginning to chant the spell.

Gasping for breath, Arden grabbed his heart and fell to the ground. He couldn't speak as pain crept into every corner of his body until he had no choice but to shift.

Bane yelled out, "Back up!" At first, the members of the Dixon pack stood their ground, until they heard the growls directed at them by their Alpha.

"Alpha, what are you doing?" Bane held his hands out to Arden, who was shaking his head back and forth. "Arden, it's me, Bane."

That's when Arden's eyes focused solely on Bane. The witch's demands echoed in his mind: *'Kill Bane. Kill Bane.'*

Chapter 15

Quinn stopped and shifted back into her human form. "I smell magic."

Jade shifted back. "How can you smell magic?"

"I just can. We need to hurry, Jade." They both took off running through the trees, toward the back of the pack house. When the backyard came into view, Quinn used all of her strength to run faster.

She'd heard that life went by in slow motion during horrific events, and what she was watching fit in that category. As they crashed through the woods into the backyard, they saw Arden shift and leap into the air toward Bane.

She screamed, because she didn't have enough time to cast a spell, but before he could reach Bane, Arden's wolf slammed into the ground.

She looked over at her brother, who had his hands up. He'd just saved Bane's life, and most likely Arden's too. She ran over to him and dropped to the ground in front of him. She could barely speak from the stress of almost losing her mate.

August knelt down and hugged her. "Quinn, I thought…"

"I know. Thank you for saving him." Tears fell down Quinn's face. "I…I love him, August."

"I know you do." August rubbed circles on her back, trying to soothe her as she cried.

Quinn swallowed hard, then pushed her brother away.

"The witch and Alpha are here somewhere. We have to find them to break the spell!" Jade yelled, getting her pack's attention.

Bane rushed forward to his sister, hugging her. "You're okay. Thank God."

August helped Quinn up. "The witch is here; we have to find them, August. She cast a spell on Arden and she has to be close to do that."

"Okay, let's get the pack together." August let Quinn go as Finley rushed forward and yanked her toward him. It happened so fast that she didn't have time to yell out before he wrapped his hand around her neck, holding her still. As he started to squeeze, Quinn's vision blurred.

August inched closer, but Finley squeezed harder. "I don't think so."

"What are you doing, Finley?" August shouted. She could see the fear in her brother's face. He couldn't do a spell for fear Finley's hand would squeeze in response and break her neck. He was that strong, and it wasn't him in control.

"He's under the witches spell too," Jade said as Finley's hand tightened further cutting off her oxygen. Before she blacked out, she felt a jolt to her back, and Finley toppled forward falling down on top of her. When she pushed Finley off and turned around, Police Chief Deaton Egan was holding his gun in his hand.

Gasping for air, Quinn crawled over to where pack members were holding Arden down to the ground. She closed her eyes and broke the spell that Hannah had put on him. She watched as Arden's wolf shimmered and he shifted back to human form.

Quinn rubbed her hand down his arm, making sure he was okay. His body was covered in sweat, but it didn't matter. She thought she'd lost him forever, and she knew now that she wouldn't be able to live without the arrogant control freak. "Arden, are you okay?"

"Quinn." Arden's voice was rough, and just above a whisper as he hugged her.

"I didn't know if I would get back in time." Tears fell from her eyes. "Arden, I love you."

When she pulled away from him, she could see the anger in his eyes. "Who hit you?"

"It was Hannah, the witch. Oh God, Arden, it's Beatrice Hoffman's sister and brother. Hannah is the witch, and her brother is the wolf who bit me and Finley. It's revenge, Arden. They want to make you pay. They're here on Dixon land. They had to be close by to hit you with that spell."

Helping her up, Arden held her body close to him. "I'm going to kill them." Quinn shivered when she heard the intent in his voice. She could tell he was still shaky from the spell. It took a lot of magic to keep an Alpha wolf under for that long.

"I hate to interrupt this reunion, but we need to find them," Bane commented. Before Arden could say anything, he gasped. Peg and David Patterson were in pain, and he could feel it. He clutched his chest and muttered, "They're in Peg and David's house."

Arden had to be the one to kill the wolf. He could have killed his mate. His witch sister was definitely going to die too. August was right when he said that Beatrice was bad to the core, meaning she had no soul and only knew how to do evil. Apparently the whole family was evil. No wonder the daughter wanted to become a wolf. She wanted what her family couldn't give her.

They didn't sneak around to the back of the house; Hannah and Silas knew they were coming. Arden knew the Death Hunters were following, waiting to see what he would do. They would step in only if Arden didn't take care of the matter, and he planned to do exactly that.

"Wait, Arden." Quinn and August held hands and silently did a spell. When they were finished, Arden kicked in the door. Hannah and Silas were each holding knives to David and Peg's throats.

"You're no match for me, Alpha," Hannah laughed. She started chanting, but when nothing happened she sneered and looked over at Quinn. "What did you do?"

"No magic on Dixon pack land, bitch." Quinn smirked. "Oh yeah, and just for your information, no magic ever in your case. You will die here; that's a promise. You're no match for me, even in human form."

Quinn knew her words would provoke Hannah enough that she wouldn't be able to stop herself from taking on the challenge.

Hannah's eyes blazed. Quinn could actually see the craziness inside of her.

"Ah, Quinn?" August leaned over and whispered in her ear. "Did you not get the memo that this bitch is crazy?"

"Yep, but I can take her." Quinn smiled.

"You think you can take me? Well, let's just see." Hannah pushed Peg forward as they all backed outside. When Hannah was out far enough, she pushed Peg to the ground and launched herself toward Quinn.

The knife was sharp as it dug into Quinn's arm. The pain made her grit her teeth, but she couldn't look down to see how bad the damage was. Hannah grew up hard, and Quinn knew she wouldn't fight fair, so looking down or showing she was in pain wasn't a good idea.

Quinn didn't have to look down to know that Hannah had cut her arm open, anyway. She cleared her mind of what-ifs; she needed to focus on killing Hannah. That was the only way to make sure this threat never occurred again. They were the last of the Hoffman line, and she had to make sure no offspring would ever threaten the pack with evil again.

Hannah lurched forward, giving Quinn the opening she needed. The move she used was taught to her by a human self-defense instructor. Using Hannah's forward momentum, she grabbed ahold of her arm, twisting it backward. Then she jumped up and wrapped her body around Hannah's like a snake, bringing her crashing to the ground. Before Hannah could twist her body around, Quinn had the knife out of her hand and to her throat, slicing it open. As brutal as it was, Hannah would have done worse to her, and at least this way she was dead.

Silas screamed in rage as his sister died. He was so caught up in his fury that he dropped the knife, shifted, and charged Arden. His quickness even caught Lennox and Cosmo off-guard. Silas's wolf was just as dirty as his human form. Black coal dust was matted into his fur as the wind blew the smell of rotten eggs up their nose. Arden had no choice but to grab ahold of the wolf and sling him against the trees.

Silas nipped his arm as Arden changed, and both wolves went head to head in midair. Quinn couldn't tell who was winning, because both wolves were biting and fighting each other so fast, and she was terrified of Silas cheating somehow.

But Arden was faster and bigger, and easily got his teeth deep into Silas's throat. She could tell that Silas was not going to give up as Arden held on tighter, crushing his wind pipe. Then he shook his head until his teeth tore further into Silas's throat, ripping it out.

Arden spit the chunk of flesh onto the ground and shifted back into his human form. Quinn rushed to his side and held onto him. His body was covered in blood and sweat, but it didn't matter. They were free from the threat.

Chapter 16

The pack gathered around the Alpha pair. "You saved my life, and I'm indebted to you, Quinn." Peg came and stood beside her.

"No Peg, that's just what friends do for each other," Quinn told her.

Peg grabbed her hand and smiled. "Yes, yes it is."

Lennox and Cosmo dragged an unconscious Finley over and dropped him on the ground. Lennox drew his sword, but before he could do anything with it, Peg, David, and Quinn all jumped in front of him.

"No, you won't hurt him." Quinn stood, holding her hand out toward the Death Hunters.

"You'd condemn an innocent man?" Peg asked. Lennox stopped and stared at her. "This is an innocent man, who like Arden's father was condemned for his actions while under a spell. You saw with your own eyes that Finley wasn't himself and was being controlled by the witch. If he dies then you might as well kill me too, because I'll not stand for it." Peg sat down in Finley's lap and wrapped his arms around her. The whole pack loved Peg and David. As they watched her forgive Finley, they all moved closer and gathered around Finley too, protecting him.

"Shit," Lennox muttered.

"Watch your mouth, young man," Peg cautioned.

Cosmo's eyes widened, and then he started chuckling.

"Yes, ma'am." Lennox blew out his breath, then put his sword back behind his back and walked off.

Arden walked up to Finley and put his hand on his shoulder. "Welcome to the pack."

*****

"I could have gotten you all killed," Finley protested.

"But you didn't, and you wouldn't let her hurt me. I could see you fighting that spell, and I knew you were going to help us," Peg answered. "The Alpha tried to kill too, but he fought it as well. You're pack, and you saved my life, Finley Egan. Admit it."

Finley sighed and looked over at his dad, then back at Peg, "I guess I'm pack." The pack cheered, all coming up to him and patting him on the back and hugging him around the neck.

"No guessing, son; either you are or you aren't." Deaton Egan walked up and put his hand on his son's shoulder. "You're my son and that will never change, but now you belong to something bigger and better. I'm still here for you, Fin, and I'm proud of you."

"Pack." Everyone stopped talking and looked at their Alpha. "Let's get this cleaned up. We run tonight and celebrate our new family members." He walked over to Quinn, putting his hand on her arm. "I'm not going to push you into mating with me. I know you need time."

"You don't want me?" Quinn asked.

"More than the breath I'm breathing, but I understand that it's got to be your decision. I'm here for you. I hope you'll come and run with the pack. No matter what, we've all agreed that you're part of our pack." Saying that, Arden kissed Quinn on the forehead and walked off. Quinn stood there, shocked that he'd just left without any demands. He gave her the control.

"Come on, Sis, let's get you home. You stink." August held his nose. "Plus you're naked, and that's disturbing to me."

Chapter 17

Jade ran up to the Alpha. "I am confused. Why you are letting her go?" Jade and Arden watched as August wrapped a coat around Quinn.

"Because it has to be her decision to mate with me. I heard what you said about how her dad always took her control away, and I understand that. I don't want to be like her dad and make her feel that way. I want her happy."

"Wow, I'm impressed. You look so calm," Jade answered.

"Jade." Arden stopped and blew out a deep breath. "I'm about to go nuts inside letting her leave, but if I don't do this then I'm going to lose her, and that is unacceptable."

"Well, you're making the right decision and I'm proud of you," Jade told him, then hugged him and walked away. Arden sat down at the table as Bane came over to him with a smile on his face. He knew the man would have something to say about Quinn.

"I can't believe you were going to kill me," Bane commented.

That was a surprise, he thought. "I'm sorry. You have to know that it was the spell. I was fighting it, but I couldn't stop. I'm sorry, Bane, you know I love you like a brother."

Bane snorted. "Yeah, I know, but this is going to cost you, my friend. I don't know what yet, but I'll ask for something and you have to give it to me."

"Anything." Arden laughed, then got up and hugged his friend.

*****

Quinn sat on her bed after her shower. She didn't have long before the run tonight. What had her so upset was the fact that Arden just let her leave. She didn't see that coming. Maybe he really didn't want her, and was trying to use this as an excuse to get rid of her.

She heard a knock on the door. "Can I come in?" August asked.

"Sure."

Her brother came in and sat on the bed beside her. "You going to the run?"

"Not sure yet. I don't know if he really wants me to show up, or if he was just being nice to a new pack member," Quinn answered, crossing her arms, but even to her own ears it was a stupid remark.

"Come on, Sis. That man is in love with you. He's giving you control of the decision. Please tell me you're not that stupid. I thought at least you had that much sense," August joked.

"You think he loves me?"

August pushed her shoulder with his. "Yes, and you love him."

"I do, but what if he tries to control me like Father did?"

August rolled his eyes. "Look, Arden and our father are two different types of men. They don't compare with each other. Father is an ass, and only looks out for himself, but Arden is an Alpha and he looks out for his pack. I saw that firsthand, and so did you. I don't know why we're still sitting here; I'm leaving you here and going to eat. Besides, there are some fine-looking babes in your pack, too," August joked. At least, she thought he was joking. She watched as he walks to the door.

"Hey, August."

"Yeah?"

"Wait up."

*****

August and Quinn arrived at the pack run. August made a beeline to the table full of food while Quinn searched for Arden.

She didn't spot him when she looked around, so she approached Bane. "Have you seen Arden?"

"I think he's already running. You can put your clothes over there if you want to go and find him. I think all the ladies have put their clothes there."

Bane watched Quinn's smile fade. She looked over at the table, which had a bunch of clothes on it, ran over to it and started stripping. Then she shifted and ran off into the woods.

"Why did you tell her that the ladies' clothes were over there? That has all the pups' clothes on it, and that's who Arden is with," Tate asked.

"Some people need a little push, and that woman needed a big one," Bane answered.

Quinn tore into the woods, seeking out Arden and the bitches who were most likely trying to steal him. *Not today*, she thought. She stopped and sniffed the air. She could hear something, but she didn't know what it was. She hadn't been a wolf long enough to know the difference in sounds and smells. As she walked closer she came across a clearing where Arden was playing with a bunch of cubs, jumping over logs and rolling around in the grass. She wanted to join in, but she didn't want to mess up their fun. She eased back, starting to head toward the party again. She must've gotten turned around, though, because when looked up she realized she was lost. Before she knew what happened, she was hit from the side, landing on her back. Alice had her pinned down, and was about to wrap her jaws around her neck when Quinn rolled, knocking her off.

Apparently, the sound of two wolves fighting drew the pack in, forming a circle as they watched Quinn and Alice go at it. Only one could be Alpha, and Quinn and Alice both knew this.

Alice had a lot of fights under her belt, but Quinn knew how to fight too. She watched as Alice tried to herd her in the direction she wanted, but Quinn wasn't having it. She wasn't going to let Alice control this fight. Jumping toward her, Alice nipped her hind leg, drawing blood. She got back up and could almost see the smile on Alice's wolfish face as she watched her limp around.

She wanted Alice to believe she was hurt as she glanced up to see Arden watching from the side. The look on his face said it all; he was worried that she wouldn't win.

Now it was time for payback—time for retribution for Jade, and the Outcasts.

She gave her a sign that she was hurt, which sent Alice lunging forward leaving her left flank open. *Big mistake, bitch.* Quinn ducked and jerked around, sinking her jaws into the top of Alice's neck. Blood oozed from her mouth as Quinn held on and tightened her grip, driving her teeth further into Alice's neck.

She needed to end this, but Alice was a fighter and clawed at her, trying to maneuver her body and get Quinn to release her. What she did next was a shock to everyone; Quinn held on and flipped Alice's body over hers, then wrapped her jaws around the soft part under her neck and sank her teeth in deeply, making Alice go deathly still. She didn't want to kill Alice, but if she didn't give up and yield she would have no choice. The pack went silent as Quinn dug her claws into the underbelly of Alice's stomach, making the wolf undergo more pain and humiliation. Alice was done for, and she knew it. All Quinn had to do was yank and her throat would be ripped out. But Quinn's wolf wanted to show who was Alpha, so she dug in deeper and continued to claw harder into her.

The whining from Alice's wolf brought Quinn back. She was so close that she almost jerked, sending a message to the pack, but Alice was yielding. Arden came over to her and put his hand on top of her fur.

"She's given up, Quinn. Come back to me, baby." Arden's sweet words were like magic to her ears. All she wanted was to be with him. Releasing Alice's neck, Quinn backed off and licked Arden in the face, then shifted.

Arden immediately picked her up and carried her away. He didn't say anything for a few minutes, until he asked, "Why were you leaving?"

"I was just letting you play with the pups. I wasn't leaving-leaving. I can't leave you," Quinn whispered.

"What? Did I hear you right?"

"Maybe."

"Maybe. Well what if I told you that if you did leave then I would hunt you down...because I love you, Quinn Lamone."

"Good, because I love you too, Arden Dixon."

Arden couldn't stand it anymore. He needed his mate, desperately. His desire for her made his actions harsh. "All I want to do right now is fuck you. I'm desperate for you, but I'm afraid of hurting you."

"Don't be. I need you just as bad." Quinn reached up and grabbed his neck, pulling him down to her lips.

"Were you worried about me?" She asked.

"Yes. I was worried that you would kill her and then regret it," Arden answered, then bent down and licked her nipples, biting down lightly.

"That feels so good."

"It's going to feel better." Gently, Arden laid her down on the ground and opened her legs. Rubbing his finger against her clit, he found that she was already ready for him. "You're so wet."

"Just for you," Quinn whispered.

Arden grabbed her feverishly, flipping her onto her knees and pushing his erection against her.

"Mmm," she moaned out. Pushing back, Quinn rubbed against him.

"Quinn, I'm holding on by a thread here." Arden gritted his teeth as his playful mate teased him.

"Then do it." Quinn purred like a kitten. Her voice was music to his ears as he slammed into her.

Catching her off-guard, Arden circled his hips around, pushing farther inside of her. The sounds she was making were pushing him to want more and more from her. He could scent their lovemaking and knew others were in the woods tonight and would smell it too. He didn't care; tonight he was making her his. She was his mate, and he wanted everyone to know.

He could feel everything inside him tense up as his orgasm raced forward. Flipping her onto her back, Arden pulled her up against him and licked her shoulder. "This is the place I'll mark you and make you mine." He didn't have to wait long before Quinn was screaming out his name, and Arden latched on and bit down into her warm skin. Her blood flowed into his mouth, and it was sweeter than anything he'd ever tasted.

Without warning him, Quinn grabbed his head, then turned it and bit into him. Even though she was in human form, she had some sharp teeth as they sunk into his neck. He pumped a couple times more inside of her, then cried out his mate's name. He could feel the bond snap into place and marveled at how solid it felt.

Arden held on until she released him, and then he looked into her eyes. "I love you."

Quinn's eyes filled with tears, but he knew she loved him too. He didn't need to hear it anymore; he could feel her emotions as he pushed into her again. He would never get enough of his mate.

Chapter 18

It had been two days since the death of Silas and Hannah Hoffman. The store opened back up on Tuesday with crowds from the big city. Quinn watched as pack mates and customers shopped for great deals they couldn't get in the city. She was going to take advantage of that, and get artists to put their work at her country store. Jade was already getting a name for herself with her Jade Cross line of purses and jewelry, which were selling like wildfire blazing through a dry forest.

But what she found odd was the fact that the Death Hunters hadn't left town yet. In fact, every time she had seen the Alpha of the Death Hunters, he was around or near Jade. She got a kick out of watching the biggest man she'd ever seen blush when Jade looked at him. Maybe there was something there, but poor Jade was so overwhelmed with orders that she didn't pay it much attention.

Arden had arranged for Finley to build a small structure on Dixon pack land for Jade to have her workers sewing and making jewelry. It was a great idea, and so far she'd hired ten ladies to sew her purses for her. She would continue coming up with designs, and ensure that each and every purse met her expectations. Jade didn't know it yet, but she was going to be a huge success. Once New York and other big cities found out about her line, they would all want it. Pack members would have jobs, and the small town would grow which is what they needed if the pack were going to meet potential mates.

"Hey baby." Arden snuck up behind her, wrapping his hands around her stomach and kissing the side of her neck.

"Hey." She pushed her butt against his erection, teasing him.

"Don't make me spank you for being bad," Arden said, then groaned a she pushed against him again.

"Did the Council agree for you to keep the women and children Silas and Hannah had in the caves?" Quinn asked.

"For now. He said that they might have to move some of them to other packs. But right now we're working on my old house and letting them live there until the Council decides." Arden started kissing up her neck.

Quinn watched as Lennox made his move and started walking toward the counter. Jade's customer had finished making their purchase and walked off, leaving Jade alone. "Watch, Arden." Lennox was about there when another woman stepped up and asked Jade to show her something from inside the case.

Lennox made an about-face and slunk away. This time he left the store. "Did you see that?" Quinn asked, excited.

"He's a Death Hunter, Quinn. Do you really want your best friend to hook up with him?" Arden asked. "Plus, she would have to move, and that ain't happening."

Quinn turned around and looked at her mate. "I didn't think about it like that."

"I wouldn't think they were true mates, anyway; she doesn't even look at him." Arden wiggled his eyebrow up and down. "Let's go to the back room and lock the door."

"I swear, you are too much." Quinn laughed.

"No, what I am is a mate who wants his woman. Come on." Arden pulled his mate into her office and locked the door.

*****

Jade looked up when she heard Quinn giggle. She could smell her best friend and now new Alpha making love in her office. She wished she could find someone who looked at her like Arden looked at Quinn, but nobody would. They couldn't get past the scar on her face, and she was just too shy. Bending down, she propped her head up against the counter and stared out at the customers. When she looked out the window, she saw the face of a man who was intently gazing at her. She blinked a few time before she realized it was the Death Hunter, Lennox Bartley, staring at her.

The End

I'm pleased to announce a new multi-author project called 'Bite of the Moon.'
This collection of shifter romance features some of your favorite authors and stories that follow heroines and heroes as they are turned into shifters. Books in the series include:

Moon's Law
By: Michelle Fox

Once you've been bitten, there's no going back.

A Night Owl Reviews 5 Star 'Top Pick!'

Kane Martin has a reputation as the tough-guy, sex-stud sheriff of Glen Vine Michigan, but becoming a werewolf has rattled him. Forget partying, hooking up with girls, and locking up the bad guys, he's got bigger problems. Like dealing with locals taking potshots at his pack, and howling at the moon in his spare time...whether he wants to or not.

And there's this girl, Charlotte. She's totally not his type, but she smells so good, Kane's not sure he can resist.

Curvy Charlotte Wills was supposed to be getting engaged and finishing up a degree in library science, but instead she's been dumped and turned into a werewolf. In the middle of trying to get her life back on track, the last thing she needs is a distraction like Sheriff Kane Martin.

But life has a funny way of going sideways when you least expect it.

Especially when you're a werewolf.

Full length novel. No cliffhanger. Features a full figured beauty who loves her curves and a wickedly sexy alpha who can't keep his hands off them.

Available at all Major Retailers

Between Two Wolves
by: Catherine Vale
Two wolves are twice the bite...and pleasure.

Recently single, Risha Reynolds wants nothing more than to escape for a weekend of hiking in the mountains. Burned by her ex, and angry as hell, she desperately needs the peace and quiet. Far, far away from the jerk who left her.

Besides, what better time to climb a treacherous mountain, and say goodbye to the world below, than after a rough breakup? What's the worst that can happen?

What Risha doesn't know, is that peace and quiet isn't the only thing she'll find when far away from civilization. She's heard the campfire stories of the beasts that go bump in the night, but Risha isn't the kind of girl that believes in myth and magic. Yet when she comes face to face with two wildly handsome strangers, she has to admit that they aren't like any others she's ever known.

If there's one thing she's certain of, it's that Colt and Jericho are hiding a secret, but when she is given the opportunity to uncover the truth, will she be willing to see what they really are?

If she opens her mind, her heart will follow...

Lyric's Accidental Mate
By: Elle Boon

A tough as nails soldier and a bad girl on a motorcycle with a bite...when they collide, everything changes.

A Woman In Need Of Saving

Lyric Carmichael is a shifter in trouble. When a pack of rogue wolves attacks her, she knows she will have to fight for her life. Being a member of the Iron Wolves MC and a wolf shifter, she's used to fighting, but with the odds stacked against her, she's not sure she'll make it out alive.

A Badass Soldier

Rowan Shade, a member of the Special Forces, has fought many battles, so wading into the fight to save a gorgeous woman is second nature. Being bitten by Lyric in order to save him from a fate worse than death, and finding out there are supernatural beings, is one of the most erotic experiences of his life. He just hopes they live long enough to explore more of this new and wild world.

A Love Beyond Reason

As Rowan and Lyric explore their new relationship, the danger to the pack intensifies. When they find out one of their own has betrayed them, the strength of the entire MC is needed in order for them all to survive.

MacBrun, Bearly a Nip
BBW Bear Romance.
By: Katalina Leon

They were made for each other, now he's accidently made her into a Bear!

Mac, is a lonely park ranger resigned to the fact there are no available female bear-shifters in Bear Clan MacBrun to claim as a mate. But his long-frustrated inner Bear refuses to take no for an answer, and makes a solo decision to claim its heart's desire.

A stormy night on a treacherous mountain road sends self-professed "boss-lady" Andi Brunell hurling over the side of a gorge and into an icy river. Mac rushes to the rescue, but fate places too much temptation in front of him in form of flirty-eyed, curvilicious Andi. The bear inside knows what's good for both of them and during the voluptuous vixen's rescue delivers an initiation-stage claim bite.

Whoops, it was *Bearly* a nip, but it was enough to set off a chain of life-changing events that flings them onto an emotional roller coaster. Mac is forced to take Andi back to the ranger's station, where she displays all the telltale signs of transforming into a she-bear. Poor Andi has no idea why she's behaving so strangely, and Mac's guilty conscience won't allow him to take advantage of her or come clean about what his Bear has done. Trying to be a good guy, Mac battles temptation until his Bear pheromones clear from her blood stream. But a long, awkward night of simmering lust punctuated by string of hilarious situations leaves both of them questioning their sanity. Once things heat up the bears come out to play.

Author's note this is a happy-for-now ending.

Meet Bear Clan MacBrun. This is the first book of a continuing series of interrelated stories, which does finish in a very happy ending for all characters introduced.

Also by Bryce Evans

The Ashland Pack
The Trinity
Big Bad Alpha

The Love of a Shifter
Once Forgotten: Twice Loved
Healing Their Mate
Destiny of Three
Destiny of Blood

Alpha City
Obsessions
Cravings

Royal Guard
Guarded Hearts

Keep up with all of Bryce Evan's new releases via her website: http://www.bryceevans.webs.com

ABOUT THE AUTHOR:

Bryce Evans is a mother, wife, and author who loves to escape to the world she has built in the Ashland Pack and other stories. She burst onto the publishing scene with a hit in The Trinity. As an active police officer, Bryce needed another outlet from the pains of others. Writing filled that void.

She loves talking to people who have the same tastes as she does and enjoys storytelling about vampires, werewolves, witches, and fairies.

She loves to read books and write about places that come together in her head. She tries to write about what she knows and usually you will find some aspect of law enforcement in her writing.

Travel with her to a world filled with vampires, werewolves, witches, and fairies were the paranormal run wild and romance blooms.

Find out more about her current projects at www.bryceevansauthor.com or follow her on:
Facebook: http://on.fb.me/1DTUd1T

Twitter: https://twitter.com/Bryce__Evans

Pinterest: http://bit.ly/1tARNSI

Goodreads: http://bit.1y/1zdRpga

Email: bryceevans12@gmail.com

Made in the USA
Middletown, DE
29 December 2017